A VINTAGE DEATH

COLIN KING

A Vintage Death is the debut novel of Colin King; the first of three Detective Sergeant Rory James murder mysteries set in Regional Victoria locations. Colin lives in Bendigo as well as spending time at the writing bolt hole he hand built in Grampians bushland. In pre-author life, he directed major government projects.

Other novels and praise
WETLAND
DEEP DOWN
WIRE AND BONE

'It's extraordinary.'
'An amazing book based around the Grampians.'
The ABC

'It's a ripping yarn, full of greed, violent death, jealousy, and a smattering of sex. Oh, and lots of wine, of course.'
Max Allen, The Australian

'Here is an author who knows and loves his Australia ... with an excursion through painful family secrets on the way to solving a baffling crime.'
Tony Wright, from The Age

'King understands perfectly Central Victoria's potential for a ripper read.'
'A suspenseful novel which is both surprising and satisfying.'
Dianne Dempsey, author, reviewer for The Age

'A great read set in a captivating corner of Australia.'
***Adam McNicol, author, The Mallee: A journey through* North-west Victoria**

A VINTAGE DEATH

This book is a work of fiction. All names, characters, businesses, organisations places and events, other than those clearly in the public domain, are the product of the author's imagination, or are used fictitiously. Any resemblance to real persons living or dead is entirely coincidental.

First published by Bendigo Publishing 2013
Published by Accidental Publishing 2018
This edition published 2025

ColinKingAuthor/
The moral right of the author has been asserted.

ISBN 9780646724768

Cover design by Daniel Soncin
Map drawn by David Lowther

Glove Box Publishing
PO Box 285 Strathdale Vic 3550 Australia
vintagestaff@hotmail.com

To Mary

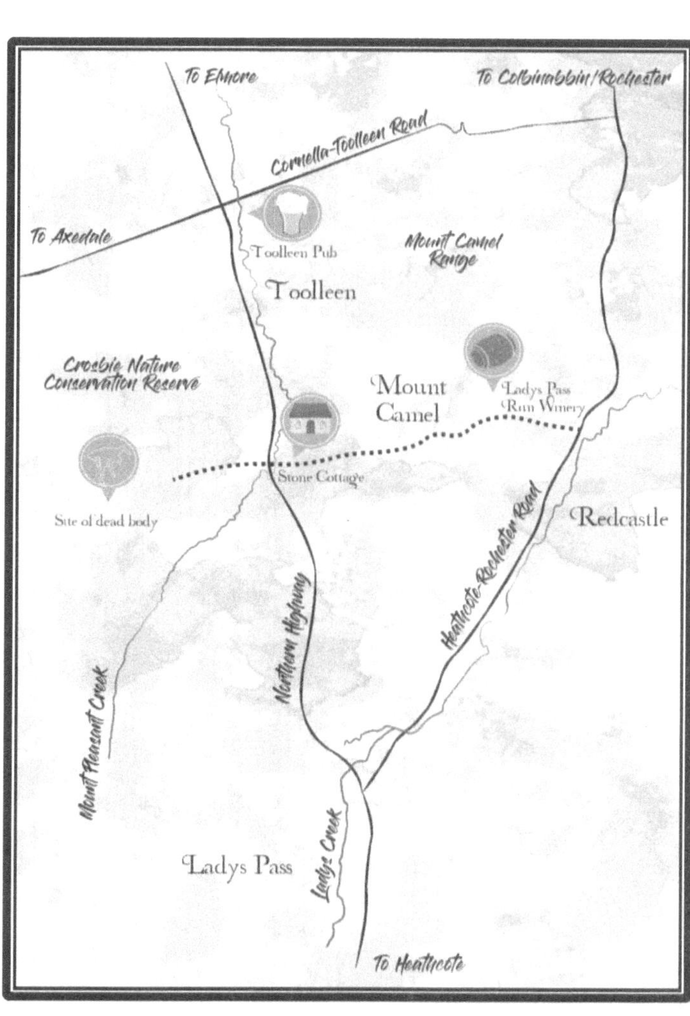

To Elmore
To Colbinabbin/Rochester
To Axedale
Cornella-Toolleen Road
Toolleen Pub
Toolleen
Mount Camel Range
Crosbie Nature Conservation Reserve
Mount Camel
Ladys Pass Run Winery
Stone Cottage
Site of dead body
Redcastle
Heathcote-Rochester Road
Mount Pleasant Creek
Northern Highway
Ladys Creek
Ladys Pass
To Heathcote

Chapter 1

Detective Sergeant Rory James weighed it up. A fourteen year void since Archie Ballantyne was killed on the day his sheep farm passed to a winegrower. No apparent motive and no suspects then — less motive and still no suspects now. On balance, it was as safe as anywhere for Rory to dip his toe back in the water. Besides, a visit to Lady's Pass Run was a perk in any occupation.

Lady's Pass. Could a place to die be more pleasingly named? In the days of Archie's demise, winegrowers around Heathcote were still appropriating such engaging localisms to adorn their cellar doors and labels. The burgeoning vigneron scene encircling the township of two and a half thousand was yet to be excised from the Bendigo wine region and proclaimed an appellation in its own right. And burgeon it did. If Archie's killer was a local, he'd have witnessed Heathcote Wine Region rise to become "Shiraz Heaven" and notch up a decade of unmissable food and wine festivals.

Its urban fringe loomed as Rory passed an archetypal row of twenty or more hobby-farm mail boxes on stalks. The wry spectacle was one of few distractions to catch his eye beyond Melbourne's northern sprawl. Ninety kilometres along the B75 had otherwise passed with sleep-coaxing early afternoon sun streaming through the unmarked police car windscreen. As an antidote, he swigged from a bottle of water, opened the driver-side window and decelerated for the self-proclaimed "longest main street in the southern hemisphere". Generations of Heathcotians had settled further and further from the centre of town without giving up a highway frontage. Perhaps that merely made it the thinnest town in the southern hemisphere.

Rory measured his progress through town by the speed restriction signs. Ninety kilometers an hour past the first stretch of scattered houses. Down to seventy beyond the house wrecker's yard and the boarded up roadhouse. Fifty loomed at the first sign of stately gold rush pubs and bank buildings. This time round, boomtown activity in the main street proper was driven by all things wine — even decaying weatherboard shops were transformed into hip eateries. Good coffee looked a safe bet.

Permitted speed crept back to sixty kilometres an hour at the retro motel. Eighty heralded the Northern Highway turn-off towards a scattering of competing wineries. Rory made the right-hand turn and was soon back to 100 amid pastures and the treed folds of Mount Ida declining to Lady's Creek. Across the bridge, the early summer vines of Lady's Pass Run, distant on the gently rising slope of Mount Camel.

'What the fuck are you doing here?' Detective Sergeant Gary Cockburn spat.

Rory halted at the door of the tasting room of Lady's Pass Run. Cockburn faced him from the un-attended counter. His face was as disagreeable as his greeting. Anyone re-creating his image with Identi-kit software would founder in search of suitably unpleasant options to click on. No set of eyes would be sufficiently spiteful, no brow so unambiguously full of menace.

But Cockburn belonged to the mob that issued the wanted posters — or at least their modern-day equivalent of grainy CCTV footage and media releases. Fellow police were thus immune to the disquiet that others felt upon meeting him. Coming across Cockburn out-of-the-blue nonetheless caused Rory to flinch inwardly.

Rory resisted firing back the same question. 'Are you stalking me?' he retorted.

'Don't flatter yourself.'

An unblinking silence hung — neither man wanting to sound more nonplussed than they were, or be first to concede an explanation for their presence at Lady's Pass Run. Rory kept his grip on the entry door. Cockburn had turned from the counter in a ready-to-draw pose — his arms hanging slightly away from his body.

It was mid-afternoon, midweek and devoid of cellar door cruisers. Cockburn seized the silence with raptor instinct. 'You should have killed him with your first shot.'

A year of therapy slid from Rory like silk off a veiled statue — his face struck rigid and voiceless with re-lived pain.

'Uh?' he finally uttered, as if awoken from sleep.

Patrick Seabridge had entered the freeze-frame from a door behind the counter. The pause on his face was fleeting but lasted long enough to show he sensed the harrowing vibration between his visitors.

'*Two* friendly policemen,' he proclaimed too cheerily. 'Which one's in charge then?'

Cockburn spoke unhesitatingly. Rory tried to breathe again.

'I'm Detective Sergeant Cockburn and this is Detective Sergeant James. I'm here about the body. I presume my colleague is here to taste wine.'

The words were polite enough but Cockburn only owned one tone.

Rory's mind swam in more directions. 'What body?' he managed to ask.

'So you're not here together then?'

'Mr Seabridge found a body,' Cockburn said forcefully to Rory. 'Hence my question: "What are you doing here?"'

'*I'm* here about the body Mr Seabridge found. What are you doing here?'

Flummoxed looks ricocheted between the three men.

'Excuse us,' Cockburn said and guided Rory out of the room with a hand on his back. He stormed onto the crushed granite car park, swung round to face Rory and hissed, 'This is fucking ridiculous. Just tell me in plain English why exactly are you here?'

Rory's response stalled on his lips when he noticed a uniformed constable alight from Cockburn's unmarked police car. He looked quizzically back at Cockburn.

'All right. I'm on a cold case. Now what's all this about,' he said gesturing toward the constable.

'Cold case? What cold case?'

'Patrick Seabridge found a body fourteen years ago. It looked like he had stumbled across a farm accident. An exploding fuel drum and fire. No enemies, no suspect and no motive for anything sinister. The local copper didn't like the smell of it though. There was no hard evidence to prove it wasn't an accident, just cop instinct that the Melbourne investigators paid little heed to. The coroner gave an open finding.'

He paused to read Cockburn's testy gaze.

'What's your excuse? Only Fran knows I'm looking at the case and even she didn't know I was coming here today.'

'It seems Mr Seabridge has stumbled across another body. He phoned Bendigo station about an hour ago.'

Detective Sergeant Rory James was a one-man homicide cold case unit. Before his recent appointment to the role, the unit was about to be disbanded after a two-year reincarnation. It had begun in a blaze of media and optimism. There was plenty of talk about fresh information, suspects, making up ground, stepping up the search for killers. And "that one vital phone call" being all they needed to solve certain high-profile murders.

Cases within living memory received full-page spreads in the weekend papers. The distance of time brought renewed public curiosity to each story. Journalists relished having a crack at something ready-packed with intrigue, despair, and pathos. It was natural fodder for the tabloid-style current affairs television shows. Plenty of old newsreel footage and melodramatic voiceovers. Advertisements for each episode featured interview grabs from surviving relatives. Their surprisingly aged faces sucked everyone into watching.

Files grew thicker from the cage rattling but none of them found a new home at the prosecutor's office. Investigators were soon being snatched from the team. The cold case unit grew cold.

Disbanding the unit was staved off when Rory returned from workplace injury leave — a euphemism for his post-shooting disintegration. Where else could they place a fragile homicide detective out of harm's way?

'Fuck,' said Rory.

'Fuck is right.'

They turned from each other, one rubbing his neck, the other exhaling audibly — inattentively taking in their surroundings as each tried to comprehend what they were dealing with.

The tasting room sat below the hill crest with a view down the final Great Dividing Range foothills to the northern plains. A sea of ripening vines gave way to straw-coloured paddocks stretching to a mirage shimmer at the base of the sky. The building's rammed earth walls matched the rich red of the soil between the vines. Its galvanised steel and glass expanses were from the Australian school of architecture. The hardwood timber deck and café tables had all greyed classily beneath a shade sail. The total package was undeniably worthy of the panorama.

The tall figure of Patrick Seabridge towered behind the glass edifice, watching the darkly suited opponents go through a silent pantomime. The sharp lines of Cockburn's suit matched his sandy, perpetually number-one trimmed head stubble. His short wiry frame was full of string puppet animation. Rory's larger physique moved with more considered thought. His careworn clobber was in sync with his dark accidently-in-vogue tousled locks. Nonetheless, a year in the wardrobe had failed to protect his suit from the march of fashion.

'Who?'

'A neighbour. Male.'

'How?'

'He said it looks like he fell out of a tree.'

'Fell out of a tree? Jesus. What was he doing up a tree?'

A distant plume of dust moved silently along the lane below.

'That'll be the ambulance.'

'Is he still alive?'

'Just making sure. Either way, your history lesson will have to wait. Let us get on with the real work.'

'The cold case is a bona fide murder investigation. And how come you happened to be at the Bendigo station?'

'I'm filling in while a couple of the Bendigo CIU blokes are doing training.' He paused, 'Didn't you say it's only a *possible* murder. Sounds like the bottom of the cold case barrel to me.'

'It could be connected.'

'No fucking way. How do you come up with shit like that? You're talking fourteen years ago. You don't know a thing about this other body. You didn't even know it existed until half a minute ago. Just piss off and let me deal with this thing properly.'

'Properly? It's just as new to you and you're already ruling things out. Coincidences don't just happen. I'm sticking around to find out what this is about.'

'You should have taken a disability super payout while you had the chance. Everyone knows what really happened. You'll be on your own for the rest of your stay in this organisation you know.'

'Play the man as soon as you're losing the argument Gary. You lasted a minute this time.'

Cockburn glared.

'I'm hanging around,' Rory added.

Cockburn cranked the glare up to eleven.

'You're wasting that on a copper. Let's see what Seabridge has got to say.'

'*I* see what Seabridge has got to say. Whatever happened fourteen years ago does not give you an ounce of buy-in for this investigation. Observe all you want but I don't want to hear you drop a silent fart, let alone breathe.'

'Have we picked a leader?' Seabridge asked cheerily when they came back inside. Rory noticed that Seabridge had come in off the tractor. His version of farm work wear was a well-worn navy-blue jumper with cotton shoulder patches and a no-longer-dressy pair of moleskin trousers. Workmanlike — but hardly a work man.

'Detective Sergeant James is with the Homicide Cold Case Unit. He's come to see you on a separate matter — the dead body you found fourteen years ago. It seems to be a habit of yours.'

Despite belittling Rory's case, it was nonetheless alien for Cockburn to forgo an opportunity to unsettle an interviewee. He paused to survey the damage.

'Archie Ballantyne?' Seabridge said as cheer disappeared from his face.

Neither Cockburn nor Rory answered.

'Homicide? There was an inquest. I thought it was an accident.'

'An open finding. The police concerns have never been put to bed.'

'I know it was an open finding but I thought that was *because* it was an accident.'

Seabridge returned his gaze to the glass wall. He combed his fingers slowly through his foppish lion-coloured hair before holding his cheek in deep thought. Cockburn and Rory waited. The ambulance arrived in the car park.

'Should I take you to Marcel?'

'Is he the new body?'

Seabridge nodded. Speech had escaped him.

'Then take us to Marcel. That's what I'm here for. Sergeant James will come back about Mr Ballantyne later in the week. Now, where exactly is Marcel?'

'I found him in the Crosbie Forest. Other side of the Northern Highway. A few k's away.'

'He was an oologist,'

'You're dying for me to ask you what that is,' Cockburn snarled.

Seabridge had regained his demeanour on their drive to the scene. He stood by the two police cars with Rory and Cockburn as the constable strung blue checked tape from tree to tree in a wide circle around Marcel's body. Leaf litter, twigs and crisp bark crunched under his footsteps. Parallel strips of eroding soil served as a vehicle track through the open box-ironbark bush. It was entirely adequate for the occasional weekend wood gatherers and trail bike riders. The ambulance man and woman were packing up and slamming doors, ready to drive the empty van back.

'A job for the government undertaker,' she said.

Marcel lay on his back. His restful posture was not the position he died in though — Seabridge had admitted to rolling him over to check that he was dead. The only blood was a head wound that matted his uncombed brown hair. The calm expression preserved on his face retained no horror of meeting death. Early thirties, Rory reckoned. Faint lines were visible on his narrow, tanned face — perhaps he was even older. A pair of multi-pocketed shorts revealed equally well-tanned legs. Marcel's slight, fit, leathery frame was built for climbing. Rory knew from the file and from a business search that Seabridge was an art dealer cum winemaker, cum restaurant partner and sometimes music festival promoter who aimed a bit higher than most. His name was associated with plenty of success stories although he seemed to have moved out of the picture before a few of those became train wrecks. Seabridge was never around to incur the wrath of disgruntled investors and ex-partners. Did that make him a smart businessman? In any case, Rory had anticipated a certain level of urbane charm — enough for Cockburn to brand him a wanker.

Seabridge sensed that Cockburn had already drawn that conclusion.

'It's a bird-egg collector, Detective *Cock*-burn,' he explained.

When emphasis was put on Cockburn's surname, it smarted. It prodded a wound that hadn't healed since primary school. 'Cock-burn,' other boys mocked with a rapid rub of their trouser fly. 'Want a light, *Cock*-burn?' His furious responses embedded a resentful disposition and permanent sneer before he was out of short pants. In his teenage years, he asked his father about changing it to Coburn, like the actor James Coburn — or at least pronouncing it Coburn. This set his father off on a rage-fuelled dissertation about family tradition and honouring the name that had fought in two world wars. His life sentence was settled. No chance of ever living in the normal world.

Cockburn had at least learnt techniques to mask and deflect the sting — this time he did it with a change of subject.

'How do you spell that?'

'Beginning with a double o of course,' Seabridge teased.

'O - o - l - o - g - i - s - t.'

'He rode his bike here,' Cockburn said turning towards the mountain bike propped against a sapling within the blue circle. 'Was that normal?'

'Marcel Chabanne was not normal. He was a recluse. He developed epilepsy from brain surgery following a motorbike accident. He wasn't able to hold a driver's licence after that. Marcel dropped out and came to live in the family weekender. It's the old stone coaching house we passed where we crossed the highway. It's been in his family since the gold rush. It began as a staging inn for horse-drawn coaches until the railway came. They kept trading as an inn for a few decades after.'

'He doesn't look old enough to be a recluse,' Cockburn said with his gaze fixed on Marcel.

'He's mid-thirties. He was a junior lawyer in Melbourne until he had the accident. The epilepsy killed his confidence and he became ultra-shy. If someone he didn't know came along while he was here, he would have hid. He was okay with the locals though. We kept an eye on him and gave him a ride if he wanted to go to town. They called him birdman.'

'Is that legal? Did he need a permit to take the eggs?'

Cockburn's question was directed with a customary accusatory glare. Seabridge folded his arms and leant back with equally-accustomed oratorial poise. He continued with studied indifference to the niggle.

'It probably is illegal but we all turned a blind eye for Marcel's sake. His grandfather was a collector when *he* was a boy. It was more of an accepted activity back then. His grandfather's collection is one of the most revered outside a museum. It's still kept in the coaching house. The historic collection fascinated Marcel when he moved there after the accident. He researched it intently. It became his passion. Eventually he began augmenting the collection with his own finds.'

Seabridge leant back acutely to fix his eyes high above Marcel and added, 'That's what brought him to this patch of bush.'

Coburn and Rory tilted their heads to the tree canopy. Three men looking skyward caught the constable's eye as he tied off the end of the blue checked tape. All four were looking upward when the conversation resumed.

'Looks like a magpie nest,' Rory said.

Cockburn shot him a glance somewhere between dismay and "Shut the fuck up". The sizable stick and grass nest was built in a fork of fine branches, beyond any limbs that looked capable of bearing human weight. The thick gnarly ironbark soared another level above the surrounding generation of re-growth trees. From no vast local knowledge, Rory gauged that this unique specimen had escaped the gold-era timber-getting frenzy. It brought to mind sepia pictures he had seen of the near-moonscapes that goldfield forests became to shore up mines and fuel steam-driven ore crushers. The ancient giant was probably spared because of its lack of long sections of trunk or limbs.

'He could go that high? Wouldn't those last few branches snap?' Cockburn said, directing his attention back to the nest. The hand held to his brow failed to stop his squinting.

'Marcel was amazing. You can see he is small and fine. He was a legend in the university rock climbing club. Fearless free soloing was his thing. That's climbing without ropes or protective harness, Detective. All he needed was climbers' chalk for grip. He tackled trees the same way. If you slip up you die, of course. But for him, an ironbark with plenty of limbs is no harder than getting up an escalator in Myers. That's why he became so good at egg collecting ... especially on his own.'

'Well this tree didn't prove as easy as you say.'

'Obviously not. But free soloing is not a method where you learn from your mistakes.'

'This magpie nest ... why would Marcel be interested in the most common bird on the continent?' Rory asked.

Cockburn gave him the ray again, less intensely this time as he turned with interest to hear Seabridge's explanation.

'A very good question Detective James. The magpie is a collector's dream. Their eggs can vary in colour infinitely. Most are light blue or green but you can also come across reddish ones, blotchy ones, even multi-coloured versions. There are three drawers full of magpie eggs in Marcel's grandfather's collection. It would be impossible for Marcel to go past a magpie nest without taking a peek inside.'

'His surname. Is he Australian?'

'Chabanne is a French name. It goes back six generations to Antoine Chabanne who came out for the gold rush. He married an Irishwoman and settled here to build and run the coaching house. As I said, it's been their weekender for decades. The family moved to Melbourne well before Marcel was born. His father is a lawyer too.'

'You're very learned on all these matters, Mr Seabridge.'

'I've met Marcel's parents. They like to think I keep an eye on him.'

'And do you?'

'He does some seasonal work for me now and again. Catches a lift into town sometimes. Other times he rides his bike.'

'Do you have his parents' contact details?'

'I do, but I've already phoned them. It's not ideal, I know, but if I were them, I think I'd rather hear the news from someone I know.'

Rory and Cockburn exchanged looks of alarm.

'And what brought you to this neck of the woods today, Mr Seabridge?'

Cockburn smiled smugly at his own turn of phrase.

'Firewood collecting, Detective.'

'Your usual hunting ground then?'

'One of them. Old trees like this are not common. They often drop good-size branches. That last lot of saw marks is mine. I got that lot about a week ago.'

He gestured to remnants of a tree canopy on the ground. Pools of sawdust between the dry leaf crowns and the trunk suggested a former limb, perhaps as thick as a cow's head. Rory lifted his head to see where the missing branch had fallen from. The others followed his gaze.

'So you already knew about this particular bird nest then?'

The question surprised Seabridge. There was a pause before he answered, 'When you look for firewood, your eyes are firmly on the ground.'

'Did you collect any wood? The Hilux looks spotless, especially for a farm ute.'

The three heads turned to look at his well-used white 1995 Toyota Hilux. It looked as though it had been given the one clean of its life before being driven to town for a trade-in price. Its myriad of tiny dents and scratches were gleaming.

Seabridge's deadpan continued, 'I had to hose it out after I collected two alpacas from Sedgwick yesterday morning. They don't travel well and they ended up shitting everywhere. It stank to high heaven. As for the chainsaw, it never got started. When I found Marcel, I phoned you lot.'

Cockburn motioned Rory to walk with him out of earshot. They retreated fifty metres along the track they had arrived on. Cockburn removed his jacket against the late afternoon warmth, then turned to face Rory in the manner of their confrontation at the Lady's Pass Run car park. Seabridge leant against his Hi-Lux and watched unashamedly as their distant pantomime resumed.

'I'll have the body collected and organise Seabridge's statement. You can continue your little archaeological assignment any time after today.'

'Is that it? What about crime scene details?'

'What fucking crime? There's a nest up there in the sky. There's ground down here. He took the short route. Not much blood, probably broke his neck. There'll be a post mortem. The pathologist will spell it out for you. Do you think someone carried him up there and chucked him out of the tree? Gravity caused this. Nothing else.'

Rory drew breath with an unconvinced tone.

'We'll be taking some photos of the scene. Don't you start making more out of this than we need to. In your condition you might prefer to be squirreled away doing paperwork, but I don't need it and nor does this case. You've come, you've observed, you've seen what happened. End of.'

'Move on folks, there's nothing to see here,' Rory mocked.

'Feeling like you're not one of us? And that's without me putting the word about. I wonder why?'

The jibes became wearisome but bearable with repetition.

'It's obvious you didn't grow up in the bush. You call it how you like. I'm taking a bit more of a look around before I jump to conclusions.'

'Well whatever conspiracy theory you and Lee Kernaghan come up with you can keep to yourself. This is not a cold case, or a hot case for that matter. As far as you're concerned, there's no case.'

* * *

Rory grabbed a camera from his car and walked further along the track they had driven in on. For the first few hundred metres, the compacted soil of the wheel ruts was too hard and dry for tyre tread prints to form. Tyre patterns were also absent in the soft silt where the track traversed the base of each gully — too sandy for tread definition. He turned after twenty minutes to see Seabridge's ute bringing a cloud of dust along the track towards him. Cockburn followed in the police car without the uniformed constable. He managed something resembling a smile and planted the foot when he saw Rory's form emerge from Seabridge's dust.

Back at the scene, the constable sat leaning against a tree and enjoying a cigarette. *At least he's old enough to buy cigarettes,* Rory thought — being no less immune to the young policeman phenomenon than members of the public. His cap had been left on the parcel shelf of the car, probably to keep his dark gel-spiked hair in order. The soft young face and easy smile invited friendliness.

'What happened?' Rory asked.

'He forgot to bring the camera,' the constable replied with an eye-rolling smirk. It revealed a shared dislike of Cockburn. An hour in the car with him would do that.

'Detective Sergeant Rory James, Homicide Cold Case Unit.' Rory said offering his hand.

'Yeah, I caught all that. Constable Caiden Logan.'

'Pleased to meet you Caiden. You'll soon learn I'm *persona non grata* among many of your colleagues.'

Logan looked blank.

'Suss,' Rory clarified.

'Yeah. I've followed your case. I'm keeping an open mind though.'

'Not yet corrupted. Give it time.'

'I think you might underestimate my generation.'

'I hope so. Anyway, I'm gonna have a look around. Take some of my own pics. No need for Cockburn to know but no need to lie if he asks you.'

'I saw you come back, get in your car and go. That won't be a lie.'

'Thanks.'

Rory began with Marcel Chabanne's bike. It was a black, multi-geared mountain bike with deep, dark-green canvas panniers straddling the rear wheel. The left pannier was smooth and empty but for a couple of still-wrapped muesli bars floating around the bottom. The right pannier was crumpled, probably from having the weight of the bike laid on it. Inside were two household egg cartons, the kind that hold six eggs. They too were crumpled. Rory opened them to find cotton wool but no eggs. Collecting containers. *What else would you use?* Rory smiled to himself. He photographed the bike, the panniers and their contents.

Rory hung his jacket in a sapling and leant the bike against the bird-nest ironbark. He photographed the trunk and then stood on the bike to photograph higher. From this vantage point he could encircle the first limb with his arms and scramble belly first onto it. There was no grace in his movements despite his six-foot frame and a few recent gym visits. The ungainly manoeuvre enabled the bark of the ironbark to live up to its name. The deep crisp ridges bit into his clothes or snapped off to exude dark red sap. His shirt tore under its unrelenting resistance and the red goo clung like Araldite.

More photographs and more shimmying brought him a knee-trembling third of the way to the nest. Constable Logan was surprised to see him photograph downward before he tackled each descent stage.

Rory reached the ground in a beading sweat. After carefully replacing the bike against the sapling, he made a wide circle of Marcel, taking portrait-format photographs that stretched from where he lay to the nest. Finally, he photographed the body in close-up detail from every conceivable angle.

'Your expenses aren't gonna cover a new suit and shirt.' Logan grinned.

Chapter 2

The suspension-challenging track from Marcel Chabanne's final landing place brought Rory back to the Northern Highway. The Commodore's right indicator beat a metronome click as he waited for two north-bound B-double trucks to thunder past the forest-track turnoff. Several frustrated sedans trailed in their wake. Constable Logan was again left to preside over the scene until Cockburn returned.

The passing bunch of traffic led Rory's eye to Marcel's stone coaching house. Its slate roof and tiny dormer windows were visible a few hundred metres to the left behind a creek line of trees on the opposite side of the highway.

He ignored his own right indicator and swung the car left. He wasn't heading for the coaching house, but the Toolleen country pub that beckoned four kilometres further on. The short wait for passing traffic was all he needed to succumb. One scotch would settle his nerves for the drive back to Bendigo. Nothing over the limit though. He would do the job properly when he got to his room.

The encounter with Cockburn reminded him just how brittle he was. *No wonder they were starting me off in a dead end*, he thought. A cold case unit in its last spluttering throes. A sanatorium for has-beens, if you believe TV shows like *New Tricks*.

Perhaps they merely wanted him to pack up the files and archive them for another five years — then someone else would regurgitate the bright idea. Cold cases had their heyday when affordable DNA burst onto the scene. Those were the desktop no-brainers. The cases that remained after the DNA revolution were cold for good reason. They began with not much and in time, the smidgens of evidence and truncated list of witnesses shrank rather than grew. Cockburn's words, "bottom of the cold case barrel", rang in his ears.

Rory drove slowly to eye the coaching house and then braked suddenly. He reversed back a few metres to be opposite the driveway. The house was some distance from the road but there was no mistaking Patrick Seabridge's white Hilux parked by the front door.

He pointed the Commodore into the entry and stopped to take it in. The windscreen vista was fronted by Mount Pleasant Creek wending its way between the highway and the front yard. Across a timber balustrade bridge, the driveway dipped around a detached billabong that fronted the house like an ornamental lake. The combination of creek-side red gums and century-and-a-half old chestnuts and firs created a European oasis of shade. The building's reflection in the black water doubled the charm. Rory crawled along in the Commodore, admiring the biscuit-tin-lid appeal. The car's crunching approach on gravel brought Seabridge to the front door.

'I suppose you're wondering what I'm doing here,' he offered before noticing the marks and tears in Rory's shirt. 'What happened to you?' he added, pulling a face.

'I walked into a tree … and as well as wondering what you're doing here, I'm wondering how you got in.'

Rory was not looking at Seabridge as he spoke. He had stepped from the car and stood hands on hips casting his eyes up, down and across the house. It was smaller than its two storeys suggested from a distance. The second storey reached into the roof space from which two small windows jutted. It was built of rubble stone in a style Rory recognised from travels in Provence. The squarest and largest of the rocks formed the corners and door jambs. A stylised horse-drawn coach was carved into the stone lintel above the front door.

A few small patches of white on the wall drew Rory's scrutiny to the slate roof — perfect in its imperfection. The uneven flat grey sheets of stones were obviously harvested from mine tailings. Wisps of a climbing plant clung to the side wall and a couple of geraniums in terracotta pots flanked the glass-panelled front door. Around the house was weed-free but not obsessively so.

'Lovely, isn't it?' Seabridge said, noting Rory's admiration.

'You haven't told me how you got in yet,' he said, declining to wax lyrical with Seabridge.

'Sorry, Detective James. Marcel let me know where the key is hidden years ago. Sometimes he was out when I came back from town with food to drop in for him.'

'And what food are you dropping in for him to eat tonight?'

Seabridge frowned as he realised Rory had not let him off the trespassing hook.

'I'm checking what his parents might need when they arrive. I imagine buying food will be the last thing on their minds.'

'Uh-huh.'

Rory walked past Seabridge and stuck his head in the front door without entering. He swung back to Seabridge and held out his hand.

'The key. And where does it go when I lock up?'

'I can show you around if you like.'

'I'll be right. Where is the key kept?'

Rory stopped Seabridge's ute as he was about to drive away.

'I'll be back tomorrow afternoon … to ask you about Archie Ballantyne. Can you be around at one?'

He waited for Seabridge to go before entering the house. Its enveloping atmosphere brought him to a halt two paces in.

Most of the ground floor had been opened into one space used as a living room combined with kitchen and dining area. A few roughly adzed ironbark columns interrupted the open plan. Old nail and bolt holes in the columns indicated prior internal walls. Another door led from the kitchen area – *only space enough for a bathroom and the back door,* thought Rory. A narrow timber stair sloped steeply from the ceiling across the back wall.

Rory's first impression was one of warmth. Bare honey-coloured native pine lining boards on the ceiling complimented the glow of the protruding red oiled ironbark beams. The stone of the entire end fireplace-wall had been left exposed. These original features were a canvas for a century and a half of piecemeal decorating by successive Chabannes. Somehow, a continuity of elegant homeliness existed from nineteenth century pieces through to a 1980s kitchen and the few modern appliances. The parchment white of the walls heightened the rightness of the furniture and wall-hung items. Even the futuristic 1950s timber chairs around the 1850s farmhouse table looked made for each other. Nothing was in fashion but nothing seemed old-fashioned. *A decorator would struggle to pull this off,* Rory marvelled.

In any other living room the egg collection would have been the first thing to catch a visitor's eye. Here, in the only home it had known, it fitted like wallpaper. The head-height chest of drawers faced the room from beneath the staircase. Twenty shallow drawers of Queensland maple were exposed by a panelled door hanging open. It resembled an overgrown architect's plan cabinet.

Rory grabbed the two turned-timber knobs of a middle drawer and drew it open. The drawer was sectioned into twenty-four compartments, each with one, two or a clutch of small speckled brownish eggs on beds of cotton wool. The drawers were numbered but each lot of eggs was otherwise unlabelled. Rory opened another drawer, lingering over the first egg collection he had ever seen. He closed the drawer and then the panelled door, removed the tasselled key holder and felt under the stair stringer for the hook it might usually be hung upon. *Ah, there it is —* positioned behind the upper end.

Rory stood back to ponder the cabinet and how it had been left open. He proceeded on a circuit of the room, checking the framed black-and-white photographs on the wall and the bits and pieces on flat surfaces. Marcel Chabanne was tidy enough but not one for regular dusting. The afternoon sun exposed a thin dust-free border alongside the inlaid timber box sitting on a low bookcase beneath the front window. The trained police eye then found other tell-tale signs of a light touch search. It looked to Rory as though Seabridge had been doing a bit more than checking tea and coffee stocks.

Upstairs was a wallpapered landing and three rooms — two with beds and one a study. The ceiling sloped down to the stone walls that rose a metre above the floor.

The exposed stonework was painted off-white and plaster filled the spaces between the roof frame. To Rory's mind, the deliberately exposed upstairs air-conditioning duct was the first noticeable clash of styles. Marcel appeared to have occupied the smaller of the bedrooms. The unoccupied main bedroom had a made double bed.

The study was simply furnished with a timber desk, a locked two-drawer filing cabinet, a modern pneumatic chair and packed bookcase. More photos of successive Chabanne generations hung on the wall.

Being a recluse had not left Marcel a Luddite. A laptop computer sat closed on the desk, but when Rory switched it on, it refused to reveal its desktop display without a password. He was forced to shut it down by turning the power off.

The downstairs 1970s bathroom was kitsch and incongruous. Rory imagined Marcel recognised it as such, because a major self-renovation was underway. He continued his unhurried inspection out the back door to find further signs of restoration. A pile of fresh slate sheets stacked beside the first stone outbuilding were ready to be chipped into shape as replacement roof pieces.

An orchard of struggling fruit trees faced stables that were given over to firewood and garden tool storage. Rory gave cursory looks inside each and continued past to the house-paddock. Beyond its fence, relics of ploughs, feed troughs and rusted machinery poked through the new season of knee-high grass.

He turned to face the coaching house. The couple of white patches that he had noticed earlier on the end wall seemed to be highlighted with distance, even though they were no larger than a tennis ball. He strode back purposefully to the lowest patch. At close quarters it was out of reach but low enough to see that it was a powdered material. The substance was reachable at full stretch standing on a weathered bench seat he placed against the wall. Rory stepped from the seat with his right hand held away from his body. He peered at the residue clinging to his fingertip and smelled it as he imagined a knowing Drug Squad detective might. At length, he ignored risk and procedure and touched it to his tongue. No cocaine numbing or chlorine taste of bleach. *In any case*, he wondered, *why and how would anyone dab whatever it was, randomly out of reach on the wall of a house?* Whatever it happened to be, it was pretty much odourless and tasteless.

As he circled the house taking photographs, Rory became aware of his own enlivenment. He was surprised to feel again the potent tonic that detection work created within him. He looked down at his ruined shirt and trousers. That first drink could wait until he got back to Bendigo, he decided.

Chapter 3

The mind can be too active when driving alone on country roads. One thought leads to another and then another. And then doubt.

Less than a week back on the job and the benefit of a year of sick leave, counselling and therapy had already been wiped. In the moment Cockburn had him alone today, he was able to wind Rory's mind back to the starting blocks. The time and effort he spent dragging himself from his pit of self-torment all wasted. How instantly images of the shooting had sprung from memory. How close to the surface it would always be.

The rest of the day passed by rote. Could he still be an effective cop or was he forever cast as an automaton going through the motions? Was there satisfaction in that? Cockburn was the first. There were plenty of others yet to be faced.

* * *

With Cockburn's prodding, the memory had catapulted into Blu-ray definition. Rory and Senior Constable Heidi Lester driving to her apartment when the call went out. Not that they needed the call, they could see the pandemonium unfolding a block ahead. A drug-fuelled dickhead, seventeen or eighteen years old, ranting with distress and waving a knife. Workers who had been lunching in the park fled screaming out the gate. Passing pedestrians bunched at a safe distance and waited for whomever to come and get him.

It was not within a homicide cop's bailiwick but he happened to be in the vicinity and so was Heidi. They hadn't had time to put the siren on when he screamed to a halt beside the small South Yarra park. Rory, pistol drawn as they ran across the grass, shouted to Heidi to use her capsicum spray.

'I've got him covered.'

Heidi's fully stretched arm kept the nozzle going. The knife holder screamed the pain off and lunged at her. He missed. Rory aimed and shot him in the right leg — almost point blank. They gaped at each other for the split second of silence created by the gunshot. Heidi recovered first. Her spray hissed again and the knife-holder's plan kicked back in. A second screaming lunge ripped open Heidi's outstretched forearm.

Rory's second, third and fourth shots were procedure perfect, straight into his torso. Signs of life lasted less than a minute.

All those homicide cases — dealing with murder daily, seeing bodies rendered lifeless by every unimaginable horror. He thought he knew as much as anyone could about killing. He had known nothing. The precise moment between a living person and a corpse is never experienced by morticians, funeral directors or homicide cops. They deal with empty vessels. This added another arrow to his quiver, albeit unwanted — an insight his peers would never know. He knew what it was like to do the act he dedicated his life to punishing. To shatter that greatest of moral principles — "Thou shalt not kill." He knew how deeply it could prey on the psyche.

The official line and media coverage had him a hero. He shot a crazed man with a knife who was attacking and wounding a female officer. The predictable outcry from righteous defenders of human rights was absent. Rank and file within the force, however, shared a view of their own. 'Why didn't he follow procedure with his first shot? Always aim at the torso. Heidi's disfigured forearm was his fault.'

Heidi took her unforgiving hurt to Cockburn's shoulder in an act of spite. Rory had confided in her about his earlier fallout with Cockburn. When Cockburn was in Ethical Standard's sights for assaulting a suspect, Rory had refused Cockburn's plea to provide a fabricated alibi. It wasn't that Rory was averse to protecting a fellow member, but his wife Lauren would have been put on the spot if Ethical Standards explored the alibi in any depth. Rory drew a line.

Cockburn created enough mitigating fudge to escape with a warning, but he wasn't the type to forgive or forget. When the shooting happened, it rekindled his bitterness. Heidi only lasted two months with Cockburn — adding fuel to his fire of resentment. Cockburn was hardly lacking motivation when he told Lauren why Rory had been driving around with Heidi.

Two relationships wrecked, an organisation-wide ostracism, a guilt-inducing shooting fuck-up and actually killing someone. Not a bad tally for one minute's work.

The Manse B&B stood proudly in the dress circle of streets that rose in a crescent on the west side of the Bendigo city centre. The late nineteenth-century two-storey mansion was a showpiece of Edwardian features. Cantilevered Queen Anne gables, wraparound verandas, balconies with elaborate timber fretwork, and Australian flora and fauna featured in the plentiful stained-glass windows. The grounds were their own miniature botanic gardens and according to the pamphlet, the place had a William Bede architect pedigree.

Ironic, Rory thought as he mounted the front steps. He was a visitor in the town where he grew up, and city-raised Cockburn had become a local, albeit a temporary one.

He hoped to reach his room before Sigrid Dobell saw him in his shredded suit and shirt.

'What did *you* get dragged through?' Her voice came from the parlour that led off the entrance hall through opened double doors.

'An ironbark,' Rory admitted, turning his hanging palms towards her in a guilty childlike display of the damage.

He held his pose as she walked into the hall, scotch in hand. The drink and her bare feet were the only concession to being at home at the end of a working day. Sigrid otherwise looked ready to slip on some heels and go out. Her makeup remained flawless, her tousle of shoulder-length blond hair in need of no more than a flick of the head in front of a mirror.

She slowly circled him with mock astonishment. The silky sleeveless blouse she wore was buttoned to a high collar and tucked loosely into a skirt. Slivers of translucent background among its leafy white-on-white design gave blurred — but not un-noticed — glimpses of bra and flesh beneath. The glow of her tanned arms also caught Rory's eye. Her dark skirt was not short but firm-fitting enough to divulge a well-kept figure.

The more he was distracted by the absence of flaws in Sigrid's appearance, the more conscious he became of his own hapless state. His tatters, the submissive posture, the wound within that he knew escaped into ever-encroaching creases on his face. While his Bakelite-brown hair had remained in situ and mostly un-greyed, the added lines on his oval face told their own tale.

It was on his spent face that Sigrid's inspection was least fleeting; daring Rory to imagine something in him appealed nonetheless.

'You can throw that lot in the bin,' she concluded.

He gave a resigned shrug.

'You look like you could do with one of these.'

She jiggled her tumbler. There was no clink of ice with the scotch.

'Thought you'd never ask.'

'Do you want to change first?'

'Not if you can stand drinking with me in this state.'

Leading him into the parlour in his scare-crow suit and her early crack at the hard stuff — Rory safely presumed he was the only guest.

Sigrid Dobell was unlucky in marriage but not so in divorces. She departed her last union with a drinking legacy and the wherewithal to move to Bendigo, buy The Manse and remodel its interior into several luxury B&B guestrooms. The weekend B&B trade was brisk and rewarding. Midweek there was the occasional hotel-averse corporate client enjoying its homely appointments.

'Bad day?' she asked as Rory collapsed into the sofa.

'I couldn't have cared if it was my last.'

'Ice?' she asked as she held a tumbler towards him.

He took the glass as it was, raised his shoulders from the sofa to take a mouthful, then dropped his weight back to feel the warmth spread into his body. He recognised her silent non-judgemental drinker's gaze upon him. Rory lifted his top half slightly for a second mouthful and said, 'I'll buy you another bottle tomorrow.'

'Let's see how far you get with this one. What are you working on?'

'Ancient murder. Years ago.'

'And it does this to you?'

'You never know, it might save me from this.'

'I wouldn't rely on that happening if I were you. You look too practised in drinking alone.'

'I hadn't touched it for months.'

'Are you all right then?' she said with alarm.

'Don't worry. It had to happen sometime.'

Rory woke to find a designer doona had been draped across him on the sofa. The bottle on the sideboard was a quarter full. His drinking prowess had slipped more than a tad, especially when he took Sigrid's contribution into account. Before he gave up, he hadn't been accustomed to waking to a bottle with contents.

When you're that good at something, you can't hide it from others. Being on the wagon became a deal breaker for him to return to work. He felt no pride in making it over the line — albeit by only a week — and leaving a quarter of the bottle untouched.

His pitiful visits to the gym had also helped his battle to resume work — the receipts covered the Workcover doctor's arse. Three months off the grog and slight fitness at least enabled him to climb a tree yesterday. He ruefully resolved to keep up the gym visits.

Nothing washed off in the shower — not the guilt, not the hangover, not even the ironbark sap ingrained in his palms. The spare suit he lugged around but never wore was the one that really needed shredding. The grey-brown disaster began life when he was best man at a fellow trainee's shotgun wedding. *At least the suit outlasted the marriage*, he consoled himself.

It wasn't consolation enough when he came to The Manse dining room for breakfast. Sigrid was in her impeccable best under the kind of bib apron women wear in upmarket gift shops.

'I liked your other suit better,' came before "Good morning".

'I'll get it out of the bin if you like,' he said with a fleeting afterthought that retrieving it and putting it on might improve matters.

She laughed warmly and leant her head with a faint smile of concern.

'I've cooked some extra eggs and bacon if you need it after missing dinner.'

'Sorry I dropped off. I haven't been good company for months. I'll try and make it up to you tonight.'

She smiled.

'Will anyone else be in?' he asked.

'Just you and me.'

Chapter 4

Driving in the morning is different. There's a new day ahead. Everything is still possible.

Take two for the cold case — beyond Bendigo's morning school traffic, heading back to Heathcote. Rory replayed his predecessor's short file note in his brain:

No consequential circumstances identified. No suspect or motive arising from the long-term distribution of the deceased's estate. No additional witnesses or evidence sources have emerged. The probability of additional witnesses existing or coming forward or of additional evidence being identified is remote at best. The probability of the death being accidental cannot be further strengthened or weakened. No action recommended.

Nine years ago, Rory drove to Bendigo to attend the farewell of Senior Sergeant Eric Clement. Eric was Rory's commanding officer when he began as a constable. Eric was also one of Bendigo's longest-serving policemen and the function spilled across several first-floor rooms in the town's grand and historic Shamrock Hotel. Rory's moment to slur reminiscences came well into the night when Eric sought him out on the balcony. Former smoker Rory had joined other nicotine desperates braving the frozen depth of Bendigo's winter. Non-smoker Eric might easily have passed for one of them with the cold visible on every breath he exhaled.

Rory was surprised when Eric had lowered his voice to a conspiratorial tone and guided him away from others. They moved out of earshot to the empty end of the balcony, overlooked across Pall Mall by the post office clocktower. Eric was shivering when he told Rory that he and a Heathcote constable were first at the scene when Archie Ballantyne died five years earlier.

Rory — who possessed a smoker's acclimatisation to being outside office buildings in the cold — was more concerned about Eric's discomfort than hearing another cop war-story. He asked Eric if he wanted to go back in. That's when Rory got the message that Eric had a monkey on his back.

'No,' Eric snapped, and straightened out of his cold-fending hunch. 'This has been eating at me for too long.'

He proceeded to tell Rory about homicide detectives being brought up from Melbourne following Eric's reading of the scene. They had listened solemnly to Eric's apprehensions without offering comment. Their indifference to his concerns only became apparent when he was led rigidly through his testimony at the inquest.

Eric had felt emasculated. Rory was his chance for redemption.

'You're in Homicide now. You have a look at it. The case hasn't been closed. I've checked on the system.'

Eric's hoarded anxiety made it sound more like a direction than asking for a favour. Rory had to remind himself that Eric was not his boss — hadn't been for a couple of years.

'No one is gonna let me spend my time on an old case. And what could I do anyway? You said there is no motive and no suspect.'

Eric sipped generously from his beer and reverted to his usual measured manner.

'Well find one, Rory. I know you're a smart cop. You stood out from the pack on your first day in the job. Just have a look at the file.'

'And what would I see if I did?'

'It *looked like*', Eric emphasised cynically, 'Archie Ballantyne had been cutting steel with an angle grinder in the shed bay where he kept drums of fuel. You know what an angle grinder in action is like — they create more sparks than a fistful of kids' sparklers. His shed had a separate perfectly safe workshop bay with a bench vice and all his other tools where he would normally do stuff like that. That's where he cut and welded steel for every gate on his farm. Why would a smart old-timer like Archie Ballantyne suddenly do something silly like that? Supposedly cut a piece of steel on the concrete floor beside a virtually unsealed forty-four-gallon drum of petrol. Utterly out of character.'

'Even if it is as suss as you say, there's no one in the frame. That hasn't changed, has it?'

'That's why it needs someone smart like you. I reckon the clue is in the truckload of fencing material Archie bought the day before. No one knew why he bought it all. His fences were all good. Either that or something to do with land. People kill for land, you know. They fight wars over land ...'

Eric stopped talking mid-thought when the post office clock began chiming three quarters of the hour. They both turned to the eerie mist-enshrouded glow of the illuminated clock face. Eric had warmed to his topic with six-pot rambling but the time-out gave him a chance to notice the cold.

'It's fuckin' freezing out here,' he yelled over the booming chimes.

When the chorus stopped on cue, he resumed his dissertation precisely where he had left off.

'... and history. Land and history, Rory. Like this place.' Eric waved his drink-free arm around to indicate the historic premises they stood within. He dropped the arm around Rory's shoulder and gestured close to his face. 'You just need to dig, Rory. Do a bit of digging for me hey?' He maintained the question with a silly head-wobbling grin that demanded an answer. It wasn't the occasion to say no, but Rory never envisaged ever making the trip to Heathcote.

And here he was, on that precise case, albeit to dip his toe back in the water — a safe excuse to go through the motions and to see if he still functioned as an investigator. Day one may have been thwarted by Cockburn but there was a silver lining. New death bled life into the old case. He wasn't sure how or why it happened, but he knew Marcel Chabanne was not another accident.

Nor was he concerned that Cockburn was treating it as an accident. That suited him fine. He wouldn't have to deal with Cockburn until he figured it out. And if he didn't figure it out, then no one would be aware of his failure. No one except himself.

The only thing to go on was Seabridge. The single common denominator. Was that enough to connect the two deaths? Was it simply a coincidence that Seabridge found both bodies? If it was a coincidence, then what was coinciding? Seabridge had twenty-four hours to hone his story about Archie Ballantyne. The element of surprise had been lost.

Kilometres ticked by and his hangover throb receded to general fuzziness. *It wasn't that long ago that a half-bottle effort wouldn't even have made it onto the scale*, he thought, wondering if this was a bad thing or a good thing. He leant to check his brown eyes in the rear vision mirror. No redness or puffiness, just some squinting he could put down to the bright morning sun. He drank from a bottle of water, then straightened his long body in the driver seat to brace himself for the day ahead.

The McIvor highway climbed out of the Campaspe River valley at Axedale and Rory took the turn off to Toolleen. The hamlet had been one of the busiest intersections of the gold rush era. Prospectors travelled from Bendigo to new fields at Rushworth and Beechworth. But that route had faded with the gold. These days it was a one car-width strip of bitumen. On the other axis, the intersecting stock route from Melbourne to Echuca on the Murray. The road bloomed into the busy Northern Highway when stock began doing the trip in trucks rather than on the hoof.

In the morning sun, the red brick pub glowed beacon-like across the paddocks as Rory approached. Its backdrop of the Mount Camel Range of hills was cloaked in the first sign of Heathcote region vines. He ignored turning left to the Lady's Pass Run and crossed the highway. A tiny general store, church, oval and a few scattered houses denoted the town.

Open Weekends and Public Holidays and By Appointment, the sign read on the stone gateway of Mount Campbell Estate. It was one of the first vineyards on the rise from Toolleen to Chinaman's Bend where the road snaked across the ridge of Mount Camel Range.

Rory turned into the entranceway. Vineyards on either side of the driveway stretched from the gate to a cluster of buildings on the rising slope. Somewhere between the two was a bloke riding a quad bike from the opposite direction. Rory pulled over, slid his window down and waved for the rider to stop.

The bike had a mini trailer in tow, full of implements, bags and plastic buckets. The helmet-less rider had a grey bearded face and, like Seabridge, he too wore his obsolete casual clothes as work wear. The white collar on his faded but fresh purple polo shirt was not yet soiled from a day's work. *Gone were the days of dun fatigues-wearing farmers with creased leather faces*, Rory thought.

Rory stepped from the Commodore and stood with his arm on the open door. 'I'm Detective Sergeant Rory James, is the owner around?'

'I'm the owner. Well, half owner with my wife. Probably less than half if you count the bank's stake. Brian Spencer.'

Rory stepped over to shake hands. Brian stayed seated on the quad bike.

'I suppose this is about Marcel Chabanne.'

'I'm on my way back there this morning,' Rory fudged.

'I'm not sure I can help you,' he said with a disappointed scratch of the head.

'Just background. I need to build a picture of the general area.'

Brian's face brightened at the suggestion that being useful was do-able.

'We've been here eleven years now. I should be able to shed a bit of light on the district, if that's all you're after. I'll head back to the cellar door if you want to follow me.'

'Lead on.'

Brian circled the Commodore with his quad bike and trailer and headed back along the driveway. Rory followed his small billowing trail of dust. They pulled into an empty signed visitor parking area. It was immediately evident to Rory that the winery, residence and the surrounding trees had all sprung out of the paddock no more than ten years ago. It was also clear that Mount Campbell Estate was more about the wine than presentation. The tasting room was a modest timber add-on to a giant gum-leaf green Colorbond shed where the real business was done.

The tasting room's interior, however, was more worthy of the shed's produce, its centrepiece a counter-top of a single slab of light coloured timber. A range of about eight wines was on display on shelves behind the counter.

'Coffee? It's real, I'm having one,' Brian offered and he busied himself behind the counter firing up a small commercial espresso coffee maker. He seemed pleased to have the excuse.

Rory sauntered hands in pockets to look at the wall-high wine region map mounted behind two sets of tables and chairs. He quickly oriented himself with the "You Are Here" sticker and turned to face the obligatory glass wall view of the vines.

Along the end wall was an open-shelved white sideboard stocked with more bottles of wine. Rory was drawn to the large glass vase of red soil which was the sole display on top of the sideboard. He leant forward to begin reading the lengthy spiel fixed on the wall behind. Brian noticed and saved him the effort.

'That's the famous Cambrian soil. It's what makes Heathcote wine world famous,' he offered with nonchalant conviction.

'Really?' he said, turning back to Brian.

Brian raised his voice to talk above the grinder.

'It's actually the oldest soil in the country. This soil can produce the boldest Shiraz wine in the world. Growers in the Barossa and in McLaren Vale would argue of course, but they can't deny that Heathcote Region's Duck Muck rivalled Grange as Australia's most expensive red. Our wines have already achieved international acclaim, although the fame is not yet as widespread as we'd like, even locally. You need to remember that we've given South Australia over 100 years start. But we're catching up with every vintage,' he added defensively.

'And that's because of this soil?' Rory said, bending at the waist to give it closer inspection.

Brian continued talking loudly, now competing with the milk frother. The Cambrian story spilled easily off his tongue.

'It's so unique, and it's relatively scarce even within the region's boundary. It runs like a spine from the bottom to the top. You can see on the map that most of the vineyards are clustered along that thin ribbon of Cambrian soil. And when I say thin, I mean thin. The region is a long shape to begin with, but the belt of Cambrian soil is only a kilometre or two wide. Sometimes only a few hundred metres. You'll even find breaks along the chain.'

'Yeah? How did that come about?' Rory said with interest well behind what was shaping as a well-crafted coffee. So far this morning he had as good as gone without. It was Sigrid's first flaw. The filtered coffee she served at breakfast looked and tasted like boiled milk infused with brake fluid.

'From friction. There are two major north-south faults below the volcanic greenstone rock in the Mount Camel hills. These faults have been pulverising each other for 600 million years. The eroded rock, metamorphed with sedimentary rock, produces the Cambrian soil. Some of it has found its way onto the slopes below but it's not as deep there. There's nothing like it for growing Shiraz grapes. Max Allen, the bloke who writes about wine in *The Australian*, reckons he'd come to Heathcote if he ever gave in to the urge to make wine himself.'

'*The Australian* huh?' Rory acknowledged the only name familiar to him.

'Yeah. It's deep, friable, well-drained but with excellent water retention. It has some weird mineralisation and micro-organisms that haven't been figured out yet, and most of us are happy for it to never be figured out. You can't get your hands on anything more exciting for Shiraz vines.'

Brian brought their coffees to the table and looked to Rory for praise.

'Looks perfect, is the wine as good?'

'There's much more satisfaction to be had making wine. Mount Campbell '04 Shiraz is our crowning achievement. We've sold out, except for a couple of cases I kept for regular customers. I can sell you a bottle if you like.'

'Mount Campbell. I presume that's part of the Mount Camel Range?' Rory answered non-committedly.

'Yes and no. Mount Camel itself is a mere grassy rise that explorer Major Mitchell — being from Scotland — probably thought was unworthy of being called a mountain. You could easily drive a four-wheel drive over the thing. The first settlers nevertheless mistook it for another nearby peak that Mitchell named Mount Campbell. The name stuck — kind of — and the local squatter named his run Mount Campbell Station. I say it *kind of stuck*, because the accent of the squatter's Scottish overseer was so thick, it was swiftly corrupted to Mount Camel. So whatever way you look at it, it's the same mountain with *two* Scottish derived names.'

He finished the story with a proud table slap and laugh.

'Great yarn,' Rory felt compelled to say, '… and great coffee,' he added in a more heartfelt tone, noticing the rich crema adhering to his so-far emptied cup.

Brian became self-conscious of his tasting room enthusiasm. He cast a more solemn look at Rory across the cup of coffee he held with two hands, elbows on the table.

'I've got to admit, we're a pretty driven bunch, if you'll pardon the pun. But you didn't come here to find out about wine though.'

'I came to a winery hoping to find out how things operate in the neighbourhood,' Rory said and patiently sipped his own coffee as a sign for Brian to continue.

'But Marcel Chabanne wasn't in the game.'

'I understand he did a bit of seasonal work for Patrick Seabridge.'

'Yes he did. And I offered him a bit too but it's a tad too far for him to get here by bike. He can't hold a driver's licence, you know.'

'I do know,' Rory answered before asking, 'And what about his house, does he have much land?'

'It's about twelve acres, whatever that is in hectares. The house belongs to his parents. It's been in the family since it was built in the gold rush. They might not want to keep it though ... not after this.'

'Does it present a good opportunity for anyone?'

Brian rested his chin in his hand and gave the question thought before answering.

'Commercially speaking, it's too small for a decent vineyard. Its history and charm would make excellent shopfront or café premises, but not where it is, even with the highway frontage. Out here it would probably remain a residence. Tree changers perhaps.'

'What about Patrick Seabridge, would it be useful to him, being at the turnoff to Lady's Pass Run?'

This question caused Brian to fold his arms and scoff, 'Only aesthetically. His plans for Lady's Pass Run are much grander.'

'What plans are they?'

'I'll leave it to him to tell you about his scheme for world domination.'

Rory was forced to put his rising inquisitiveness on hold. Through the window behind Brian, he noticed a woman walking toward the building. Her short-sleeved pale blue shirt had the winery name woven on the pocket. A thick brown leather belt was threaded on her blue jeans.

'I saw you had company,' offered the blonde woman as she entered. 'I'm Helen.'

She was of similar age to Brian. Rory was left to assume she was Brian's wife or partner.

'Detective Sergeant Rory James, I'm here about the death up the road,' Rory said, allowing them to think he meant Marcel rather than Archie.

'Oh! Not sure how we can help there,' she said, sounding both anxious and alarmed.

'I'm just finding out about the area from Brian,' Rory offered, to take the frown off her brow. 'He was telling me that Patrick Seabridge has grand plans for the area.'

Brian and Helen exchanged glances before Helen took the baton. 'If you haven't heard already, Patrick Seabridge has a proposal to build a mega wine tourist centre on his property and the idea has not gone down well with everyone.'

Helen took a seat at the table as she spoke — beside Brian and opposite Rory.

'By the sound of it, you're not among those in favour of the idea.'

'That's because most, if not all of the wineries at this end of the region are boutique wineries. If you come to the Heathcote Wine and Food Festival in October, you'll see more than fifty of us circling the showgrounds. All of them are small wineries like this. All devoted individuals, couples or family concerns. The wines are also individual — handcrafted by different winemakers with different philosophies and techniques. Different ways of growing, harvesting, pressing, filtering, watering ... or indeed not watering — different everything.'

She was counting the list off on her fingers. Brian watched her, nodding, like someone planted beside a politician being interviewed on camera.

'And then there are the subtle differences in microclimate. We're on the western side of the range. Our grapes ripen a week after those a few kilometres away on the eastern slope. We're not as hot as the northern growers just twenty ks away but we miss most of the cool breezes the southern end gets off the Mount Macedon Range.'

Having completed her earnest discourse, she leant her forearms on the table and asked Rory, 'Do you know about wine, Detective James?'

'It's a bit like art to me. I know what I don't like,' he told her.

'Well despite all these variations, every maker's wine is unmistakably Heathcote. Seamless, inky, full-blooded reds.' She was warming to her topic. 'And they're so exciting — chocked with enticing nuances you won't taste in reds from less temperate areas like the Barossa. That's what we think the region's strength is. That's what we should build on. We're a wine version of an arcade of specialty shops. The last thing it needs is Patrick Seabridge's colossal homogenous supermarket plonked in our midst.'

Helen could not disguise her disdain when she mentioned Seabridge's name.

'Isn't there anyone doing it on a bigger scale?'

'I must admit there are some big boys operating within the region but they don't intrude on the smaller wineries' world. They stick to the northern area where the irrigation water is laid on. No cellar doors — just an address that allows them to put "Heathcote" on the label. Seabridge should take a leaf out of their book.'

'Did you know Archie Ballantyne?' Rory slipped in.

'Archie Ballantyne!' Helen said with some astonishment.

'Has that got something to do with Marcel?' Brian asked more coolly.

'I heard that was an accident,' Helen said.

'There was an open finding for Archie's death. The Homicide Cold Case Unit happens to be having another look at it. Not because of Marcel Chabanne though.'

The word "homicide" cast a sombre tone. *Good, it's out there*, thought Rory. *That should get around the winemaking world soon enough. Gotta start making waves sometime ... See what washes up.*

'We never knew Archie. That happened a few years before we moved up here from Melbourne,' Brian said gravely.

'In fact, we looked at his former property before we bought this. The people who purchased it after his death were re-selling. You probably already know that Patrick Seabridge bought it. It adjoined his property, so he was more willing than us to pay what they wanted.'

'And that was about nine years ago?'

'Nine years next month. I remember Heathcote had just seceded from Bendigo to become its own autonomous wine region. We missed all the angst that went along with that. But thank goodness it happened. They had such a distinctive wine identity to begin with and the Heathcote Region brand has just kept blossoming. Oz Clarke's *Australian Wine Companion* describes drinking them as ...,' he paused to recall the quote exactly, '... like watching a fat man with twinkle toes excel at the Blue Danube Waltz.'

Rory managed a limp smile.

'Sorry, I'm off on my favourite subject again. We heard a bit about Archie when we were looking at buying his place. He was a local sheep cocky whose family had the place for generations. He was a widower when he died and the property was sold by people on his wife's side of the family. I don't think he had kids or any surviving rellies on his side.'

'And Patrick Seabridge bought the property?'

'One hundred hectares of it, including the homestead. He put in some more grapes and runs a few alpacas on the rest.'

'What's his wine like?'

Helen and Brian exchanged looks as they had done before answering Rory's original question about Seabridge. Again, it was Helen who answered.

'Brian won't speak ill of a fellow winemaker, but at the risk of sounding like sour grapes — that's a common winemaker's joke — there are local growers who don't think the taste matches the price or the hype. In fact, many think it is a very un-Heathcote-like wine.'

'Why do they think that? Does he do things so differently to others?'

Helen stroked her neck as she began by qualifying her answer.

'If I was to hazard a guess … and I don't have any proof, so this is an off-the-record remark … I'd say the product emerges from Patrick's process as an average wine and he ends up bringing in others to perform a bit of post-production wizardry. That's what it tastes like to me.'

'And winemakers can do that and get away with it?' Rory asked, well recognising a familiar vein in the way people perceived Seabridge.

'You can get away with it if you have friends in the media. He's a part-timer like most of us and his day job is as an art dealer. Journo friends seem to come with that territory, so he manages to get plenty of over-glowing reviews for his wine. He boasts about how he can use those contacts to promote the region for us all.'

'What I'm hearing is the locals think he's a wanker.'

'I wouldn't be unkind enough to call him that,' Brian chipped in.

Helen cocked her head and fixed Brian with a protracted wry smile.

With the topic of Seabridge demonstrably spent, Rory rose to check out the sale wines behind the counter.

'Before I go, I *will* grab a bottle of the '04 Shiraz you said you have stashed away.'

Chapter 5

So-called progress versus the old way cf doing things, professional jealousies, intrigue, an us-versus-them divide. *Only the profession changes with each murder,* Rory mused as he exited the Mount Campbell Estate driveway.

If you think you have problems, then try killing someone, he countered in his mind. Even when it's something you've given thought to and been trained to face, you don't know how you will react and how you will be affected until it happens to you.

Most cops think about it from time to time. Well at least the Victorian ones. Rory joined the force when its practice for dealing with armed threats who failed to heed warnings was to shoot several times to the torso. It was never referred to as shoot to kill, not within the force, but it certainly wasn't easy to portray it otherwise.

Before the mid-1990s, Victoria ran rings around every other state when it came to the number of people being shot by police. More than a couple every year. At the time,

Rory was involved in the joint Victorian and NSW operation dealing with Italian organised crime. It was an era when NSW cops sported a "bent" reputation. One joint briefing he attended became legendary in police circles. A high-ranking NSW officer addressing the meeting is reported to have said, 'We won't steal anything … if you don't shoot anyone.'

Despite Victoria Police's then record and reputation, officers involved in shootings usually had scant repercussions to be fearful of. The media unit and the Commissioner would generally come out in support and any subsequent investigation was conducted by the police themselves. The public weren't too concerned if it involved hardened criminals, but the demographic was changing, especially with deinstitutionalisation of psychiatric patients. The need to always shoot to kill was being questioned more and more.

"Alternative conflict resolution techniques" were introduced — things like capsicum spray, less shouting, standing off and Tasers. The number of police shootings diminished but the likelihood of it happening never went away, especially with the rising phenomenon of "suicide by cop".

Every incident on the news played in Rory's mind. Surely shooting to kill was a last resort for an experienced cop. The Wangaratta woman with a knife didn't die. She was dealt with using capsicum spray before being shot in the leg and shoulder. Those cops wouldn't end up on the nightly news, walking stony-faced into and out of an inquest. Wasn't that a job well done? Rory regularly attended the firing range. In his own mind he was as disposed and as able as anyone to stop a knife-wielding assailant in their tracks without killing them.

And when it happened, a shot in the leg wasn't enough. Heidi's gaping arm produced blind rage that replaced thought and training. Or perhaps the training automatically took over. Perhaps he should be grateful for that. Either way, neither was ever factored into his conscious thinking. His own second, third and fourth shots took him utterly by surprise.

The quickest police action of his life became his longest lasting. He tried to please every side of the argument and ended up pleasing none. In one fell swoop he lost his wife and his lover — neither of those recoverable. His kids — both lost for now, but that might change. And the career he was clinging to? He thought he at least had one handhold on that — until yesterday. Now he rated himself a day-to-day proposition at best.

Rory pulled the handbrake on, stepped from the Commodore and walked slowly into the bar of the Toolleen pub.

'Beer?'

'You're a day too late with that offer.'

'Yeah? So what'll it be today?'

Barmaid antennae detected gloom that she didn't need to hear about. Not that Rory looked like the type to dump it on her, but she wasn't the type to take that chance.

'A Coke, no ice, please,' Rory said as he scanned the chalk-drawn counter lunch menu above her. 'And the rissoles.'

Rory took a stool at the bench set against the front window at the opposite end of the bar to the pool table. He nodded to the only other customer — a craggy local farmer dressed in tractor garb — tackling the rissoles with a beer at a table beside the window bench. Rory turned to the window. The flat paddock scene was intermittently blotted out by close-up 100kph passing traffic. *Pubs of inner Melbourne are more restful,* he concluded.

The headline of the folded *Heathcote Times* caught Rory's eye. "Local man dies in forest accident". He scanned the article. "Lady's Pass resident, Marcel Chabanne ... descendant of the original settler of the coaching house ... believed to be visiting the Crosbie Forest alone when he fell from a tree ... body discovered by neighbour collecting wood ... no suspicious circumstances". Polite and respectful of a fellow local.

'You dealing with that?' the farmer asked him.

'Why do you ask?'

'You're a cop aren't you? Been asking questions at the Mount Campbell Estate.'

Christ, he thought. *The whole place is monitored by bugs and sophisticated CCTV for real time transmission to everyone in the field. Or is that just a hearing aid he's wearing?*

'Don't miss much, do you? I'm Detective Sergeant Rory James.'

A bone-crushing hand shake.

'Cornell Freeman.'

'Mr Freeman. You a farmer round here?'

'Yeah. A real farmer. Mainly sheep. My place backs on to the forest where they found him.'

'You must have known Marcel then. A bit of a shock I suppose?'

'You could say that. Found by Seabridge. He was the one that found Archie Ballantyne too. More than ten years ago now. Did you know that?'

"Seabridge" had been said with some distaste.

'I suppose you knew Archie too?'

'In the fifties we played footy together in the local Mount Pleasant side. We saw a fair bit of each other after that when our wives were alive. It's a long time ago now …' He lapsed into glazed thought.

'Did you ever wonder how Archie came to be cutting steel near the petrol drum?'

'I didn't have to wonder long. There's no way he would have done that. It was no accident and that Bendigo copper knew it. Homicide Branch came up from Melbourne. They wouldn't know their arse from a hole in the ground.'

'Even so, the case was never closed. The "accident" finding was never completely nailed down.'

'Well, fat lot of good if that's the case. Nothing ever came of it.'

'Well, I'm actually taking another look at the case now.'

'You're looking into it again? How can you do that after so long?'

'I'm with the Cold Case Unit. That's what I do.'

'What? Like "New Tricks".'

Rory feigned a cringe face.

Cornell Freeman cocked his head in amusement.

'That's good. That's good,' he said. 'But I don't know where you'd start. I told them what I thought at the time. Archie would never have done something so dumb. Never.'

'What about the load of wire. Do you know why he bought that?'

'Has that got something to do with it, then? The Bendigo copper asked me about that. 450 yards of fencing and a gate. I didn't run into Archie so often by then, so I didn't know what he was up to. It must have been something internal though. All his boundary fences were in excellent nick. They still are.'

The barmaid called to Rory that his rissoles were ready.

'Can I buy you another?' he asked Cornell Freeman as he went to the bar to collect his meal.

'Thanks anyway, but I've got some sheep to get into the yards before the truck comes this arvo. Next time, hey.'

* * *

The brown tourist road sign to Lady's Pass Run appeared a few hundred yards short of the coaching house. Rory slowed enough to notice a blue Golf in the driveway. Marcel's parents, he assumed.

Chapter 6

It was Rory's second visit to the Lady's Pass Run winery but he was seeing it for the first time. Yesterday's events rendered his first impression a blur. Even before his encounter with Cockburn he had failed to notice the weekend-only trading hours signposted at the front gate. Had Seabridge been at his day job in Melbourne instead of discovering Marcel Chabanne's corpse, then Rory's surprise visit might just as easily have surprised only himself.

His morning visit to Mount Campbell Estate added perspective that was absent the previous day. Lady's Pass Run had a sense of arrival from the moment he turned from the Northern Highway. The gravel lane rose slowly alongside the imposing grassy hummock of Mount Camel to an entranceway of sweeping concrete walls with understated stainless-steel signage. Its arty, brutalist design would not have been out of place fronting a Silicon Valley IT park.

The driveway climb continued among vines to the striking building nestled on a commanding shoulder below the summit. The building exterior leapt from his memory at first glimpse. The interior however, remained a mystery.

The tasting room was no front door add-on to a winemaker's cherished Colorbond mega-shed. This was a designer showpiece worthy of fine art. Outbuildings were discreetly out of sight along the approach road. Nor did any tarnish the view through the front wall of glass, or the couple of picture windows that framed vineyard views.

Seabridge had switched on the elaborate internal lighting despite it being a non-opening day, presumably in anticipation of Rory's visit. The empty place was indeed a gallery of sorts — or at least the chamber to the left of the counter and cafe space was.

The large high ceilinged, windowless alcove glowed with scattered pools of light highlighting wall and pedestal-mounted exhibits with less-is-more minimalism. The pervading white surfaces were interrupted at the far end by the exposed rammed earth wall.

Rory was about to enter the gallery space when Seabridge replicated his entrance of yesterday. Today's moleskin trousers were a dressy pair and his tailor-made navy-blue check shirt was tucked in. Rory was reminded of the look rural politicians favour when being filmed for an interview on Sunday.

'I like your other suit better,' Seabridge said, succeeding in putting him on the back foot. In his dated backup suit, Rory felt like he was valet parking a Datsun 180B.

'Me too. But the trousers sacrificed themselves in pursuit of the truth.'

'You know the truth?' Seabridge said with some disquiet.

'Not yet. Not as far as Archie Ballantyne is concerned.'

'But what about Marcel?'

Still uneasy.

'What about Marcel?'

'I mean … is there something new?'

'Detective Cockburn is dealing with that *accident*. You'll need to ask him.'

'Right,' said Seabridge and lifted his chin in thought.

'I see you've brought your art world ethos to the vineyard,' Rory offered to end the un-Seabridge-like silence.

'Not entirely. In fact there is only one piece of art in this small collection. Let me show you around.'

He stepped over to the first white block pedestal to explain the two discreetly lit bottles on show.

'These are the first bottles of the first Lady's Pass Run vintage.'

The display notes quoted from a *Bon Vivant* review. "Mouthfilling voluptuousness".

'But this is not the first produce of Mount Camel, and I don't mean the squatter's sheep. No, *this* put the place on the map before they even had maps.'

Seabridge gestured theatrically to the wall-mounted display case of Aboriginal artefacts. 'There's an Aboriginal stone axe-head quarry on the eastern slope of the mountain. It's well over 1000 years old. The greenstone is perfect for producing a ground-edge tool that could be used for everything — cutting trees to get possums and honey from hollows, stripping bark for canoes and shields, clubs, butchering large animals — all sorts of things. These were valuable items they traded near and far. A Mount Camel greenstone hatchet head like one of these could turn up anywhere across Australia.'

Rory stepped closer to inspect several axe heads, drawings and text on display.

'The one with its handle still attached is ultra-rare.'

Its authenticity was obvious from the grimy patina.

'What about this bigger rock with a groove worn in it?'

'That's a grinding rock. They used those to shape the edge.'

Seabridge was on his game. Any concern about Rory's purpose evaporated when his well-practised fervour of elucidating knowledge to impress a visitor kicked in. In his eagerness to astound, he stood too close and held the listener's eye too intently. Each close-up dissertation ended with a questioning smile that commanded a suitable response of wonderment. Rory moved to the next exhibit to gain some personal space.

'This is our pièce de résistance. It's even older. Melbournopterus. It's the only known specimen in the world. The fossil was found in the forest below here in

1953. This is not the original of course, that's held in the Melbourne Museum. But this is a plaster cast that wasn't supposed to be taken.'

Rory looked at Seabridge in a disbelieving way before turning back to examine the forty-centimetre specimen. It was nearly twice the size of a human head. Indeed, the relatively flat casting resembled a cloth face-covering into which menacing eye sockets had been stitched. The suggestion of nose and cheek bumps and hair-like tuffs along the upper edge capped off its sci-fi humanoid appearance.

'It's a relative of the King Crab. Those smaller stones are actual chert fossils from around here'

'And this Melbourn-op-terus thing, it's the only one in existence anywhere?' Rory marvelled as he read and pronounced the name slowly.

Seabridge nodded eagerly with his smile firmly fixed.

'I know. This place should be famous without the wine. There's even copper and silver in the ground. Check out these.'

He glossed past the second Lady's Pass Run vintage display.

'Green jasper gemstones. These particular specimens were found at Lady's Pass itself. That's the lower ground between Mount Camel and Mount Ida range. Spiritualists say they have healing powers.'

'How come it has the name Lady's Pass?'

'It was named after Margaret Hyde, a widow with young children who purchased and ran Mount Campbell

Station before the gold rush. The pass ran through the western corner of her pastoral run. Local folklore also has it that a gentlemanly bushranger in the area would "let ladies pass".'

Rory leant forward to better see the polished and unpolished stones. They prompted him to ask, 'You don't seem to have any of the red Cambrian soil that other local winemakers are so proud to put on show.'

'Ah, you've done your homework Detective James. But alas, I have to say you have not seen the wood for the trees. This whole exposed rammed earth wall is made of Cambrian soil — and some colourless binding agents of course. This card tells the Cambrian soil story.'

He pointed to a small gallery card that sat forlornly on the rammed earth wall — its tiny print only able to be read by one craning person at a time.

'Impressive,' Rory admitted out loud.

'But this is where the Cambrian soil story really begins with me.'

Seabridge turned Rory to a triptych of frames on the opposite wall. The first frame held two black-and-white pencil sketches of vineyards. The middle frame exhibited several pages of an obviously old hand-written letter in French. The third frame contained a printed English translation.

'Do you have any interest in Australian history?'

'I only recently found out that Blaxland, Wentworth and Lawson was not a firm of solicitors.'

'And you're in charge of the cold cases — tch tch. What about Australian art?'

'You mean like Rolf Harris?'

'Now I know you're taking the piss. But you might like to hear this story anyway. It's the reason I purchased the land from Archie Ballantyne.'

'That was going to be my first question.'

The police purpose interrupted Seabridge's self-satisfied raconteur manner. 'It's not an incriminating story,' Seabridge retorted.

'Don't take my interest as an implication of anything. I don't even know if we need a suspect to close this file. The inquest finding was open. At this stage I'm simply interested in finding out about the area — what makes it so special. And look how easy you're making that for me. I'm standing in a room dedicated to the place.'

Rory signified with spreading arms and a half swivel.

'Indeed, it does mean a lot to me Detective James. You'll realise just how much when I tell you the whole story. Do you fancy a tea or coffee? It's not a short tale.'

Rory jumped at the chance to sit down and escape Seabridge's up-close delivery. He took another tour of the displays while Seabridge disappeared behind the counter. He was examining the two pencil sketches when Seabridge emerged carrying the teas.

'It all began with that top sketch,' he nodded in Rory's direction. Rory gave it a perfunctory second glance and joined Seabridge at a table in the café space.

'A Mrs Merchant came to our family's art dealership with that very sketch almost twenty years ago. She thought it might be a Buvelot. You will see that it is signed *"pour BUVELOT"*.

'Before you ask, Louis Buvelot is the grandfather of Australian landscape painting. That's the view of Frederick McCubbin no less. Other Heidelberg School artists who studied under him, like Tom Roberts and Arthur Streeton, regarded him as their true forerunner. Their works were all typified by Buvelot's pioneering *plein air* tonal impressionism. Buvelot himself studied in Lausanne and then in Paris with Camille Flers. Flers and his *paysage intime* contemporaries were the "open air realist" predecessors of impressionism.'

He noticed Rory fidgeting with a sugar sachet and hastened to encapsulate his point.

'Before you glaze over completely Detective, Buvelot's contribution to Australian art cannot be underestimated. He was originally from Switzerland but he also had a career in Rio de Janeiro before gaining greatness in Australia.'

'I promise not to underestimate,' Rory assured him unconvincingly.

Seabridge continued un-fazed. 'What also excited me about the drawing was that it was supposedly left to Mrs Merchant's great grandmother by Madame Buvelot herself. Caroline-Julie Buvelot lived in Melbourne another fourteen years after her husband died. When she passed away in 1902, she distributed her husband's works among her friends. This gave excellent provenance to Mrs Merchant's drawing.'

'I sense a "but" already.'

'You're right. I quickly recognised that this was not a Buvelot, although it turned out to be something equally interesting. Look, I'll show you.'

They walked to the drawings.

'The bottom drawing is a reproduction of a Buvelot pencil sketch.'

It featured a briefly outlined and shaded farmhouse among gum trees and a mid-ground of what may or may not have been rows of vines. The foreground clumps of grass were even more ambiguous.

Seabridge continued, 'The most obvious style trait is the absence of sharp detail. This is typical of all Buvelot's sketches. He used the pencil broadly and softly to create an image with light and shade.'

He demonstrated with broad air-pencilling motions in front of the sketch.

'Now take a look at Mrs Merchant's drawing above. By comparison, it could almost pass as a pen and ink. There's no mistaking the vines, individual leaves, the trees, the brow of the hill. You can see that a trained eye is not needed to spot the difference. Can't you?'

He delivered his enthusiastic close-up invitation to respond directly into Rory's face.

'Uh huh,' Rory said quickly.

'Exactly!' Seabridge confirmed like a Eureka moment.

'Mrs Merchant had to accept that her great-grandmother's drawing was not a Buvelot. We both assumed from the notation "pour Buvelot", or "for Buvelot", that it was given to Buvelot by someone else, but there was no way of finding out who. I did some research but the drawing was not in a style that could be matched to artists acquainted to Buvelot. The picture was nevertheless old and saleable. In the end, I bought it from her at a dealer's price for an unknown work of the period. She left disappointed but with fair recompense.'

The tall figures stood shoulder to shoulder and continued to look at the sketches as they spoke.

'It doesn't sound like you were *too* disappointed,' Rory said with un-noticed cynicism.

'Not at first. It was far too heavily framed, probably because the family regarded it as a Buvelot original. It needed something more modest to make it appealing to my clients. I discovered this letter when I removed the backing paper from the original frame. A French letter as some smutty visitors like to say.'

Rory had not yet read the translation on display. With piqued interest, he turned to Seabridge and asked, 'Could you read French?'

'No. So the first thing I did was have the letter translated. It turned out to be from a French friend of Buvelot called Claude Gatineau. Gatineau was a writer and photographer who also dabbled in painting. From what I could find out, he and Buvelot first encountered each other early on in Paris among a bohemian coterie of romantic writers and naturalist school artists. They were briefly re-acquainted years later in India in 1855. Buvelot had by then returned to Europe from Brazil but was unsettled and missing the warm climate. He and artist Ferdinand Krumholtz took the trip to Calcutta to paint. Gatineau was en route to the goldfields in Victoria.'

They made their way back to the table as Seabridge continued.

'Gatineau spent a couple of years on the Bendigo diggings without making a fortune. During his time in Australia, he supplemented his income by drawing, painting and experimenting with the new medium of photography. He also ran a café in Melbourne for a while. Ultimately, he had no outlet in Australia for his true love of writing and he returned to France. Eventually he had plays performed in Paris.'

'It all seems a long way from Mount Camel,' Rory said, reminding Seabridge of the question he was addressing.

'Sorry, Sergeant. I'll get on with it. Most people find this fascinating,' Seabridge added without seeming slighted. He drew breath audibly and picked up the tale in Central Victoria.

'We know from his letter to Buvelot that Gatineau travelled from his Melbourne café to Bendigo and met a squatter in the Shamrock hotel. When the squatter found out that he was a painter, he asked him to accompany him to Deniliquin and paint his homestead. From what

Gatineau says in his letter, the whole experience was one he preferred to forget.'

'So then he came here?' Rory asked impatiently.

'Well, yes. But it didn't just happen. If you let me tell the story you'll see that there were other circumstances at play.'

The hurt tone drew an apologetic grimace from Rory and a gesture to continue.

'In his eagerness to escape Deniliquin, Gatineau took the newly opened Telegraph Line of Royal Mail Coach. Instead of returning to Melbourne via Bendigo, this particular coach service took a new alternative route through Echuca, Heathcote and Kilmore. And that brought him to the last staging stop before the McIvor diggings — as Heathcote was known — to the coaching inn owned by Antoine Chabanne.'

Suddenly a link … however ancient. Suddenly Rory's interest was unfeigned.

'What? A forebear of Marcel?'

'Don't get too excited Detective, this is still only the beginning.'

'Go on then,' Rory conceded, and downed the last of his tea.

'Like Gatineau, the young Antoine Chabanne came to Victoria for the gold rush. His family were vignerons at Condrieu in the Rhône Valley, not that far from Buvelot's home in Switzerland, as it happens. I found out that Antoine was eighth in a family of eight that would have been doing it hard. At the time, there were grape crop failures and soaring land prices. Antoine would have had nothing to lose and everything to gain by venturing to the goldfields.

'He nevertheless hedged his bets in two very crafty ways. He sailed from Marseilles with his family's best wishes and a hefty supply of their best Syrah grape vines. That's the European name for Shiraz.'

Seabridge was back in full storytelling flight. He backed his chair further from the table as his hand gestures grew.

'While at sea, he discovered that as a non-British citizen, he would not be able to own land unless, and until, he became naturalized. This may have been why Antoine found himself a wife when he travelled from Port Melbourne to the McIvor diggings. He met Brigid O'Connell working in her uncle's inn at the Irish stronghold of Kilmore. She came from Tipperary as a young single female assisted emigrant. For some reason, Irish females outnumbered Irish male emigrants in those days. He must have possessed irresistible French charm, because she accompanied him on the remainder of his journey.'

Rory found himself nodding responsively to Seabridge's magnetic voice.

'His priority, of course, was to get his vines in the ground. You will see in Gatineau's letter to Buvelot that Antoine rode to the top of Mount Camel to survey the area for a suitable location. He didn't have to gaze beyond the mountain-side itself. He struck vigneron gold on this very piece of land. He described it as "God holding a mirror to Condrieu." The surroundings matched his family's French domain in every detail.

'The only drawback was its distance from Heathcote. But once Antoine had seen this place, any other site was out of the question.

'The land was held as a pastoral licence and he persuaded Archie Ballantyne's ancestor to sub-lease this twenty acres to him. Within months, he and Brigid also acquired the coaching house block in her name — to be close to the vines.'

'Hang on,' Rory finally interjected. He moved his cup and saucer aside to lean forward. 'Archie Ballantyne? You mean they, he and Marcel Chabanne, were connected that long ago?'

'Fascinating, isn't it?'

Coincidence appeared worryingly *un*-coincidental. There was no sign of the story ending and it already included Chabanne, Ballantyne and Seabridge. The storyteller ignored Rory's furrowed brow and continued with unabashed enthusiasm.

'It was some years later when Gatineau pulled into the coaching house and sat down for a meal while the horses were being changed. He was overwhelmed by the tiny slice of France created by Antoine, and by the chance to talk at length in his native tongue. It was the height of summer and the house garden was full of vegetables, chooks, eggs and fruiting plum trees. His host transformed it into a meal worthy of La Maison Dorée. It was everything Gatineau was disdainful of *not* experiencing in his encounter with the Deniliquin squattocracy.

'When Antoine poured Gatineau a wine, he refused to believe it was not imported. To settle the argument, Gatineau stayed the night and was taken to this very spot the next morning to see the vineyard. He was so taken by the experience that he did the actual sketch you see there on the wall.

'When you read the letter, you will see that he sent the sketch to Buvelot to encourage him to come to Australia.'

Rory couldn't help fast-forwarding a century and a half.

'Were the vines still here when you purchased the land from Archie Ballantyne?'

'Good heavens no. The Victorian wine industry was decimated in the 1890s by the phylloxera virus. The vines would probably have been uprooted and burnt,' Seabridge said indifferently. He was eager to return to the crux of the story.

'The site melted back into the grazing landscape without leaving a trace. But that's the great thing about Gatineau's sketch. The surrounding detail is so good that I was able to identify the exact spot he had placed his easel. The drawing showed me exactly where Antoine planted his vines — the precise paddock. We're standing in it as we speak … or we would be if we weren't sitting down.'

Seabridge delivered the last sentence with a performer's verbal flourish, and then reached for his cold, untouched cup of tea.

His satisfied smile was not reciprocated, however. Rory put his hands behind his head and looked ponderously at Seabridge.

'Another long story short … here I am,' he volunteered to Rory's silence and took a wincing sip of his cold tea.

'And that's when you turned your attention to Archie Ballantyne?'

The short story began to grow.

'Not straight away. By that time I had become casually interested in the early days of the Heathcote winemaking renaissance. The early renown of Jasper Hill and Duck Muck labels could not be ignored by informed wine followers. And there was an art connection with Len French. He's the artist who did the colossal glass ceiling in the National Gallery of Victoria. He visited the Rhône Valley in the 1970s and also recognised the suitability of Heathcote soils for growing Shiraz. He moved here and began Mount Ida vineyard. They called it "French's folly" because Shiraz was well out of favour at that time. They were ripping them out of the ground in the Barossa.'

'But Shiraz is not uncommon these days.'

'It's been around for centuries, of course. Hermitage in the Rhône Valley is the home of Shiraz. The full-bodied Rhône Shirazes were once used to improve feeble wines from the more high-profile Bordeaux and Burgundies.

One hundred years later, the might and the worth of Shiraz was being rediscovered at Heathcote.'

Rory surprised Seabridge by taking a spiral notebook from his pocket and flipping it open on the table, ready to make an entry.

'And did Archie Ballantyne know all this when you bought the land from him?'

Seabridge appeared not to miss a beat but the raconteur edge dropped off.

'I didn't need to tell him. The Cambrian soil thing was no secret by then. I didn't get the place for a song, you know. The thing with Archie was whether he was happy to sell at all. He procrastinated for nearly a year before I wore him down. And don't take that the wrong way. I had no axe to grind with Archie. I went to see him on settlement day with champagne and beer to celebrate our deal. That's when I discovered his body. The cork was never popped.'

'I hear you've acquired more of Archie's land since his death.'

'Not straightaway. I couldn't afford to for a good few years. I had debt on this bit of dirt as well as all the vineyard establishment costs. We bought it when it came back on the market about ten years ago. Archie's in-laws had sold it on in the meantime and it had nothing to do with him by then.'

'Does the new bit of land include the shed where he died?' Rory asked as he jotted a note. Seabridge looked distractedly about the room before answering.

'It was the original house block. Archie replaced the homestead in the 1950s after white ants ate the old one. The workshop and shed are on the same block. After the fire, the new owners re-built the shed on the existing scorched concrete slab.'

'And you wanted that property for more vines?'

'You've probably heard that we have a large development planned — an art museum winery resort.'

'Who is the "we" you're talking about? Are you married?'

'I have a partner, Ursula Ryman, but we're not married. When I say "we", I'm referring to the development consortium we are both part of. The whole thing is being done on an enormous scale.'

'Tell me about that.'

'Is it relevant? This is fourteen years later. Everything has moved on.'

'You would hope so, but accidents are still happening.'

Seabridge stared bemusedly at Rory and stood.

'Look, I have to head back to Melbourne now. The bones of the thing are on our website. Why don't you take a look at that. If you have any questions about it, I'll be back at the weekend.'

'Okay Mr Seabridge. I'll see you on the weekend. This thing has waited fourteen years, a few extra days is do-able.'

Seabridge continued his questioning look at Rory for too long before shaking his hand goodbye.

'Okay Detective James. Make it late afternoon when the punters are heading back to town.'

'Before I go, do you have a copy of Gatineau's letter? The English version.'

Chapter 7

Road time. Lady's Pass to Heathcote. Heathcote to Axedale. Axedale to Bendigo.

Weekend work, hey? A chance not to return to his single man's flat in Melbourne. The 1950s-built domicile with its cell-like solid concrete internal walls. His son, Nick, had made his first awkward visit about a month ago. Rory wasn't holding his breath for the follow-up. Nick's sister, Steph, would come round and come around but it was still early days for her. There was no one there to miss him. No pet, no paper, *"no cigarette"* he sang in his mind with an incongruous leap to Roger Miller's *King of the Road*.

A few days of tourist mode might be just what I need. As long as he didn't bump into Cockburn. *Maybe Ashman's Men's Wear still operated and I could buy a new suit from Carlo. Was his name Carlo or was that the bloke at Adleys? Maybe Silvio was still cutting hair.* All the obvious things he should have done for his first day back.

They were easy to see now, but he had too many mountains to climb at the time — staying off the grog, getting off the sertraline, other people, thinking. Maybe he would have handled Cockburn better if he had bothered to spruce up. However, it was his encounter with Cockburn that brought the added intrigue of Marcel Chabanne's death. That's where he sensed real re-empowerment. If Chabanne's death was related to Ballantyne's, it would be the first development in the case for fourteen years. Had the undergrowth parted to reveal a trail? Was broader restoration afoot? The personal satisfaction that comes with a start, a middle and a finish.

The whole Ballantyne-Chabanne thing ran too deep to be a coincidence. Getting the stuff onto a whiteboard was his second train of thought. It couldn't be done at the Bendigo police station, especially with Cockburn stationed there. Not even back in Melbourne. He had to get a hold on this somehow — find out how Chabanne's non-accident might be linked to Ballantyne's non-accident. Then he would break the irrefutable news to Cockburn that no one climbed the ironbark tree other than himself. He would save and savour that pleasure.

'Drink Rory?' Sigrid Dobell greeted him from the parlour.

'Not just yet Sigrid, I've got some correspondence to read. Here's a good red I found today — Mount Campbell Estate Shiraz.'

The use of Christian names felt novel to both of them.

'Thank you. Maybe we'll get a chance to share it before you head back to Melbourne.'

'As it happens, I need to stay on over the weekend. Is the room still available?'

'Not the one you're in. I can give you the single room next to the library though, if it's not too small for you.'

'A bit of a come-down, isn't it? Going from the four-poster to a single bed. Can I use the library too? I have a bit of work to do in the morning. I might need some sticky tape and paper.'

'Help yourself to whatever you find in the cupboards.'

'Anyone else in tonight?'

'No. They're all turning up tomorrow.'

'Then do you mind if I take you out for a meal … to make up for bombing out on you last night? Is there somewhere close we can walk to?'

Chapter 8

My Dear Friend Buvelot,

How much pleasure it gives me to write to you, however abundantly my penned French may be marred from disuse, for I have found no audience for my former profession since the moment I boarded the Mazagran at Bordeaux. I say this with the least sum of regret however because my adventure among the new Argonauts, although unyielding of a Golden Fleece, has not been otherwise without reward.

I tell you this as attestation of Australia as a meritorious destination. Here, the discomfort that the winters of Neuchatel now impose upon your health will take flight. The summers, like those known also to Naples, bring sunshine to the colony of Victoria for eight months of the year. Once again, you could enjoy a warm climate such as you once knew in Rio de Janeiro.

My reflections to you are imbued with a recent and most remarkable encounter with a compatriot. I should however first tell you that meeting fellow countrymen so many leagues from Greenwich is neither frequent nor rare. Indeed, the colony's Lieutenant-Governor La Trobe, who returned to England before my arrival, is of French lineage. I mention the recent Lieutenant-Governor because he was educated in Neuchatel, where I hope this letter finds you, and it was there that he also met his Swiss wife. This may not be such news to you as many of Madame La Trobe's friends and family have been enticed to emigrate here.

And yet, the colony's Neuchatelois, like its Frenchmen, are without the everyday reminder of their homeland that Melbourne is to its English residents. To think one is at home and to speak at length in sweet French is a pleasure denied at every public house, shop, and church. This I discovered when I left the diggings behind me after two years, intending to return to that great capital of the arts and my good friends of yore. But instead of boarding the Mary Shepherd, *I decided to invest the modest auriferous savings yielded to me from the Bendigo diggings and founded the Café des Mines in Melbourne. Although this name honours my medley of gold digging companions, my café was created as a corner where foreigners could sit in comfort and rendezvous with their countrymen. The surroundings I laid out and the fare I offered to my customers fashioned a window where they might glimpse France again.*

For the while that I prevailed as a good café-keeper, I was patronised by shop-hands, labourers, merchants and artists alike. The painter Nicholas Chevalier was a regular visitor and friend, although his landscapes are overly romantic for my own eye.

It was not from the provisioning of others that I espied my own nostalgic vision of France however. That occurred upon the recent farewell journey I took to Bendigo diggings. It is there that I met a "squatter". This word is used for the sheep breeders to whom the government granted rights to immense pasturage holdings of thirty or forty square miles. They live on isolated stations where they accumulate the largest fortunes in the colony.

The squatter I met in Bendigo was returning from the sale of his fleeces at the Port of Geelong and he was a fellow guest at the Shamrock Hotel. Upon learning of my humble ability at painting, he asked that I accompany him to his station near Deniliquin and complete a portrait of his homestead. It is not such a rare occurrence that artists residing in the colony are asked by squatters to paint the fruits of their prosperity. I have painted more than several myself, for, although French writing is not of saleable demand, painting speaks a universal language.

I accompanied the squatter northward into New South Wales to the most featureless plain imaginable. It was saved in its habitability only by a passing stream of some size. The squatter's dismal abode was devoid of any kitchen garden, poultry or house cow. He lived almost entirely on mutton and dry bread and drank only brandy. The Englishman does not taste and will only favour wine that is fortified. To tolerably depict the squatter's residence on canvas, I took licence to embellish every feature beyond the forlorn reality it presented to me. The squatter took prodigious pleasure in my exaggerated representation. He paid me handsomely from the proceeds of his wool sale and I made haste to escape back to Melbourne.

In Deniliquin township, I found that a competing coach line had opened a new route to Melbourne by way of the McIvor diggings and through the Irish settlement of Kilmore. I was pleased to be making this novel journey and it was by this fortune that I came to the miniature France distant from France that I have already mentioned. This was at the ultimate staging inn before reaching the McIvor diggings. The inn is owned by Antoine Chabanne, who is a native of Condrieu on the Rhône, and his Irish born housewife Brigid. You would indeed recognise the rustic coquettishness of the stone inn he has constructed in the rural style of that wonderful valley that lies between Paris and Neuchatel. Its slate stone roof and verdant gardens of vegetables, fruit trees, geraniums and roses were a vision like none I have seen since the winds took me from Bordeaux. Its cultivations flourished from water drawn from the more than meagre stream winding past the front gate. The inn presented every accoutrement of civilised nourishment and aesthetic that was absent in the kingdom of the squatter.

Antoine's skill did not conclude with the creation of his physical paradise. He was able to transform the produce of his garden into rural cuisine worthy of the best patronised cafes in the villages of his homeland. Antoine is from a family of vignerons and so it surprised me when we argued about the wine he served. It was not possible for me to believe the nectar I was drinking had not been transported from France. I saw no vines on his property to convince me otherwise.

Our debate was however of a good nature and he told me that his vines were planted three kilometres away at a place where God held a mirror to Condrieu. The Syrah vines came to Australia with Antoine packed in moss and potato slices to preserve their roots.

The vision of Antoine's homeland matched the terroir of his family's vineyards in every detail. The stinging afternoon sun drops beyond the hill's brow at the same early time of day as in Condrieu, and soft breezes from the south, like the north winds of Condrieu, keep frost at bay. In summer the grapes are permitted to ripen leisurely in the clement morning sun. Antoine's El Dorado for vines sits on a rise behind the inn. It is known as Mount Camel and Antoine agreed to take me there the next morning if I would stay the night. I resolved to do so and immediately bid farewell to the coach.

I can tell you that Mount Camel is neither a mountain as we know them, nor does it resemble a camel for that matter. The vineyard however is the vision of Rhône that

Antoine had described to me. I had seen fit to bring my sketching equipment on our ride from the coach inn. I immediately set about capturing the indisputable French essence so unfamiliar to this landscape. It is this drawing that I enclose with my letter to you and hope that it is worthy of your appreciation.

Should you ever venture to live for a while in Australia then I recommend that you seek out Antoine's Rhône in miniature. It is at the extremity of the vast undulating hinterland that stretches northward from Melbourne to the plains. A painter of landscapes will find many grand and inspiring subjects that are as virgin to the brush as any blank canvas. I am certain you would also find demand for your work among those that now attach themselves so purposefully and so fondly to this embryonic destination.

I say goodbye my friend but no longer with a heart laden by the half hemisphere that lies between us. I will soon be returning to Paris and hope that it is no great time before we can again dine together at Café de Buci.

Your entirely devoted
Claude Gatineau

Chapter 9

'Did you get your emails read?'

'Not emails. An actual French letter, or at least a letter written by a Frenchman.'

Sigrid raised her eyebrow quizzically.

'Really,' he added. 'It's on display at the Lady's Pass Run. The property had a previous life as a vineyard in the 1800s. The original vines were planted by a Frenchman.'

'And he wrote letters home?'

'He probably did, but the letter I read was from another Frenchman who stumbled across what he called a "miniature France distant from France". He was overawed enough to sketch it and write to tell a fellow world traveller.'

They were seated in the bistro of the Boundary Hotel. Drinks had been served and their meal orders placed. Sigrid opted for the duck and noodle salad, Rory the lamb Wellington. The ease of familiarity — or of two drinks — had not yet descended upon them. Rory feigned interest in historic photographs on the bare brick walls as their small talk topics came and went too quickly. A local recognised Rory and said a quick hello.

'Are you *from* Bendigo?' she asked.

'I grew up here.'

'Do you have family here?'

'Not now. Mum and Dad moved here from Melbourne when they were first married. They're in Queensland now.'

'I don't think I will ever be a local. The people I meet are all passing through … which I don't mind actually. I'm getting too old to make new friends.'

'I seem to have lost all mine,' Rory said.

'Separation? From my experiences, half of them take sides and the others avoid you … not wanting to be seen taking sides.'

'Separation, ostracise-ation, everything-ation in my case.'

'I could see that last night. You sound and look like you've been through a wringer or two. When was the last time you smiled?'

'I remember when I *stopped* smiling. Over a year ago. I'll try not to tell you about it sometime.'

'But you had a better day today? Did your day go well?'

'My past got in my face yesterday and I found out I wasn't ready for it.'

Saying it out loud caused Rory to ponder his own words before continuing.

'Hey, don't get me crying in my beer. As it turns out I did have a better day. I also learnt something from the Frenchman. Like discovering pleasure in foreign surrounds.'

Rory lifted his glass in a toasting fashion to Sigrid.

She smiled and clinked his glass.

Later as they strolled the short distance back to The Manse, she held his arm and asked, 'Your Frenchman, does he have a hand in what you're investigating?'

'I think he might.'

Rory surveyed The Manse library's books as he waited for his laptop to boot.

Green River Rising by Tim Willcocks, A Bob Hawke biography, another called *Peacock MP*, a couple of Bryce Courtenay's of unbelievable thickness, something by Steve Martini, holiday titles like *The Job and Angel of Honour*, an Australian Dictionary, and a 1970s edition of *Explore Australia*. A beach-house collection he decided, as the laptop chimed that it was ready for his attention. Browsing for a night-time read would have to wait.

No personal emails. A few YouTube links from colleagues who had been too lazy to delete him from their group emailing lists. Some intranet procedural updates from various divisional heads and the latest crimes statistics delivered with a carefully crafted and patronising covering email from the Chief Commissioner.

Nothing to send.

Rory found sticky tape and some A3 paper in the built-in cupboard beside the book shelf. He joined four sheets together to create a whiteboard of sorts for his link diagram, closed the laptop and spread the blank sheets out on the library desk over a copy of *The Age* — to stop the felt tip pen marking the ancient desk. His mobile rang.

'Cockburn. I got a preliminary pathologist opinion on Chabanne.'

'Nothing to do with me, you said.'

'Do you want to know or not?'

'Want to know,' Rory replied in Cockburn speak.

'Neck severely broken resulting in death from spinal shock.'

'Is this a "told you so" call?'

'I just don't want you jumping at shadows with your cold case.'

'What shadows?'

'I spoke to Marcel Chabanne's parents yesterday. They say they had an aggressive approach to buy the place. We'll be checking it out but I can't see it altering the pathologist's finding. In the meantime, I don't want you going anywhere near the parents or whoever wants the place so badly.'

'Is it anyone connected to Seabridge?'

'Not on the face of it.'

'Just tell me you'll let me know if you find out they are connected to Seabridge.'

'If you don't hear back from me, you can take it there's no connection.'

'Did you find out when he died?'

'Dead for about twenty-four hours.'

'Anything on his computer?'

'Someone's looking at it for me.'

'Thanks for the heads up, then,' Rory said, not trying to hide sarcasm.

'I'd like to say it's a pleasure but …'

'But it isn't.'

'Exactly. See ya.'

Rory's paper whiteboard was headed by four rectangles. His simply-drawn male faces in the first three boxes were labelled Marcel Chabanne, Archie Ballantyne and Patrick Seabridge. The fourth square — an outline of a head around a question mark — represented the "desirous purchaser of coaching house". These were variously connected — or not — by lines to each other and to lower circles labelled "Lady's Pass Run" and "coaching house". The words "Marcel Chabanne's forebear" were written along a dotted-line between Marcel and Lady's Pass Run.

He Blu-Tacked the sheet to the bookshelves and stood back.

'Oh what a tangled matrix we weave,' he said out loud. He studied it for some minutes before spreading it across the desk again to add a third tier box — this one marked "Lady's Pass art museum development" and connected to Patrick Seabridge. Rory re-hung the diagram and studied it a while longer as his laptop rebooted.

'Let's see what Mr Seabridge is up to,' he told the diagram and typed Lady's Pass Run into Google.

The Home page featured the now familiar Lady's Pass Run logo. There was no mention of the proposed development under the "About Us" tab. Rory ignored the "Our Wine", "The Region" and "Contact Us" tabs and tried "News and Events". It produced a drop-down menu of several past gallery events — an upcoming concert weekend and something call "Proposed Lady's Pass Museum of Art". This led clickers to an entirely separate web site.

The new location featured a page-size computer-drawn image of Lady's Pass Run vineyard superimposed with an ultra-modern building facade of two storeys stretching around the curve of the hill. A circular glassed tower rose above the main entrance. The only text was an "Enter Site" button. This led to the page headed Lady's Pass Museum of Art gallery and resort with a dot point list — "a museum of old and new art; a 144-room hotel; a world-renowned winery; a spa centre franchise; and conference facilities catering for 340 delegates".

Rory examined its slideshow of other computer-generated images. Other links to "Consortium Members" and "Museum of Art Advisory Board" threw up "This page under construction: in the meantime, please forward an email to obtain any further information", and an emailing link.

I don't think I'll be sending an email.

Chapter 10

Behind the counter, a woman with an unfamiliar face was pouring tasting amounts of wine for a smiling grey-haired couple.

'This is the '06,' she elaborated and shot a glance to Rory. 'Would you like to taste our '06 Shiraz too?'

Rory found himself nodding yes to the smiling woman. Her teeth shone against light olive skin, her deep honey-blonde hair pulled back loosely through a wide red clasp. The casual shirt had the expensive look of a woman effortlessly dressing down for the occasion, rather than a dressing up effort.

'You must be Ursula.'

'I am,' she smiled even more broadly. 'You've heard of me? All good, I hope.'

'Only briefly, I'm afraid. I'm Detective Sergeant Rory James. I arranged to catch up with Patrick this afternoon.'

'Yes. He mentioned it. But he wasn't expecting you until closing time.'

She was unfazed at him being a policeman. However, Rory's surprise appearance caused her engaging demeanour to become less engaging. The early arrival was no accident on Rory's part.

'Sorry if I got the time a bit wrong. Is he around?'

'He's taken a couple for a look at the old cellar. He might be a while. He tends to get carried away with a willing audience.'

'I wouldn't mind seeing it myself. I might wander over if you can tell me where to find it.'

'All right,' Ursula said, still annoyed at his taking charge. 'It's a bit of a walk. Just follow the path to the right around the hill.'

The walking path reached a fork as it crossed the shoulder of the hill. The right path descended to a two-storey stone wall façade attached to the face of the hill. *Pre-twentieth century by a long shot*, Rory guessed.

The winery and cellar were obviously entirely underground. The hillside had been excavated to create an expansive forecourt in front of the façade. Its heavy timber arched doorway resembled a train-tunnel opening. Rory recognised the imposing structure from the website pictures.

The rougher right-hand path was cut into the hillside to pass the top of the façade and onward to the run's alpaca paddock.

He descended the steps cut into the hillside to the cellar forecourt. A Colorbond workshop faced the cellar façade across flat ground that had been repaired here and there with fresh granite gravel. Its open door revealed Seabridge's Hilux ute back in farm mode. Baling twine strings hung from the rail behind the cabin. Dust and straw littered the tray.

Seabridge's voice seemed to be amplified by the cellar as it met Rory's ears through the large doorway.

'The original vigneron would have gained his excavation and shoring skills from mining — or even from his homeland. He also built the stone house you might have noticed on the corner when you turned off the highway. It never gets above fifteen degrees in here,' he heard Seabridge tell his audience.

Rory listened patiently until they emerged like miners into the daylight.

'Detective James. I wasn't expecting you so early.'

'Thought I might mix pleasure before we get down to business. Your '06 Shiraz is impressive, I have to say.'

'Thankyou, Detective.' He smiled before turning to the quizzical couple. 'Do you mind making your own way back, I might look after Detective James. I'm afraid I had the misfortune of finding an accident victim earlier in the week.'

'Of course. We heard about that. And thanks for the tour. I think we'll snap up some of that '06 ourselves on our way out.'

'My pleasure. Thankyou.'

'What a massively impressive feature this is,' Rory said as they watched the couple ascend the stepped path. 'From what I heard you telling them, I gather that Antoine

Chabanne built this … and it's on the same parcel of land he leased for his vines.'

'Indeed. And yet another reason why I had to have the place. It's not just a cellar … we make the wine in here too, just like Marcel Chabanne's great, great, great-grandfather did. Come inside. I'll show you.'

The interior was a mix of the nineteenth and twenty-first centuries. Stainless steel vats and gantries sat among stone walls. The brick vaulted ceiling and adze-cut beams supported a mezzanine floor. Shrink-wrapped cardboard cases on pallets sat alongside dusty cobwebbed bottles in racks. A forklift was parked by the door.

'This seems like an enormous investment for Chabanne to have committed to on leased land.'

Rory's head swivelled up and around assessing his own statement.

'No doubt, and it would have lost all value when phylloxera struck and growers were forced to rip out their vines. After that, it made a good hay store for Archie's family.'

'Hmm.'

'Did you have a chance to check out our Museum of Art resort website?'

Seabridge leant against the fork lift and crossed his arms and a leg. He was ready to be cross-examined.

'I did. It raised more questions than I already had.'

'Oh?'

'There's almost no detail on the website. I gather it's at a very early stage.'

'Yes and no. The concept is well developed but we have so many ducks to line up behind the scenes. The council are supportive so we are assuming planning permission will be forthcoming, despite some predictable opposition. We're also negotiating with the council to seal the road from the highway.'

It was another favourite Seabridge topic and he was unable to maintain the defensive posture. His hand gestures were soon rivalling those of a conductor.

'Then there's the question of water, not for irrigation as many fear, but for the hotel and spa. We're dealing with Regional Development Victoria about extending the Cornella pipeline. It's a reliable source of water from the Goulburn.

'There's also foreign investment matters concerning the Evard Group's involvement. They are a Swiss hotel chain that are excited to be heading the consortium because of the Buvelot connection. It's not in the DNA of government bodies to respond quickly, even for the best of projects. And everyone else has their own due diligence processes as well.'

Rory was facing Seabridge from the doorway. He took a pace or two outside to a fresh repair in the surface of the forecourt and scuffed the new granite gravel. With both hands in his pockets, he looked up to ask Seabridge, 'The lack of information must surely be ammunition for your critics.'

Seabridge glanced down at the scuffed gravel and uncharacteristically gathered his thoughts before answering.

'Very perceptive, Detective. You're right, of course, but I'm confident it will sell itself when all those ducks are in line. It's a no-brainer for everyone in business in the Heathcote wine region. As it stands today, Heathcote makes the best Shiraz in the world and it couldn't be less known. Many like to think it's a boutique industry. More like a cottage industry when you think about it. Most cellar doors only open at the weekend. There's nothing here on the scale of Yarra Valley or Margaret River. People don't speak of Heathcote in those terms. Not yet. I think some of our critical fellow winemakers are scared of making money. But that will change.

'Even when they pull a crowd at the annual festival, there's hardly anywhere for people to stay. A scattering of B&Bs, an old pub or two and the retro motel. They fill up in no time flat and everyone else has to travel or stay in Bendigo.'

They had wandered a few more paces onto the cellar forecourt as Seabridge spoke. Rory ostentatiously took in the surroundings while he listened.

'I'm not the one you need to convince,' Rory told him.

'No,' Seabridge said with a sudden bothered expression. 'Do you mind if we head back? Ursula will probably need a hand.'

'Yeah,' Rory said nonchalantly.

They turned towards the path and Seabridge sprang back to life.

'Our project will put the place on the Australian map just to see the art, let alone the winery and spa. The advisory board we are lining up for the museum of art will match the NGV. The best names want to be on board because this is aimed at the level of Tarrawarra where they exhibited the Archibald, and Hobart's MONA gallery. We'll have strong links with the Bendigo art world because of their gallery's recent successes. They also happen to house the largest Buvelot collection in the land.

'You're not going to get all that in Heathcote without somewhere for a decent number of people to stay. The place will also become a conference centre of choice. Delegates will be bursting to explore the boutique wineries and eateries. The wineries won't need to change a thing. Everybody will love them just the way they are. There's absolutely no reason for anyone to feel threatened.'

Seabridge and Rory reached the brow of the rise between the old cellar and the modern "cellar-door" premises. Cars in the car park had grown to about eight. Mount Camel loomed ahead of them behind the tasting room.

'Did Buvelot ever actually come to Mount Camel or Lady's Pass?'

'He may well have,' Seabridge replied with inextinguishable enthusiasm. 'He made extensive sketching tours of Victoria, like he did in rural areas around Rio de Janeiro and Paris. We know he visited Mount Macedon and painted homesteads in the Western District. I'd put money on it that he found Gatineau's suggestion irresistible.'

'Did you know that Marcel Chabanne's parents were approached to sell the coaching house?'

'No. No I didn't,' Seabridge said apprehensively. 'Do you know who it was?'

'Not that I can say. But it was not part of your grand scheme?'

'No. You've got me worried though. It may be someone positioning themselves to piggyback on our proposal. The place is pretty much our front gate. It adds charm just by being there. I wouldn't like to see someone do something tacky there.'

'So it would be in your interest for it not to be sold.'

'That would depend on what was planned for the place.'

'And if you owned it, nothing unwanted could be planned.'

'I hope you're not trying to make something of it. There's plenty of other land along the lane where we're exposed to that kind of risk. But honestly, it's not rated as likely. Having said that, I'll still be making my own inquiries.'

'Good luck.'

Chapter 11

Saturday night alone in a B&B. Sigrid was there but not there. She fluttered in anxious flight around the house attending to what her guests may or may not care enough about to mention when the booking website prompted them to do an on-line review. *She's not even having a drink*, Rory lamented to himself.

He eschewed his small single room by the library — its wall-mounted TV set made it too prison-like. Scotch and the morning papers in the parlour would have to do. He was good at doing "alone".

Most of the weekend guests had come to Bendigo for a wedding. The only other couple had seemed too young to return to The Manse this side of midnight, but they bumbled into the parlour at ten, loosened by a flirty meal and an arms-around-each-other stroll home that verged on foreplay. It was hard for Rory to know who was supporting whom as they wobbled smirkingly into the parlour.

The sight of a man quietly drinking on his own had a sobering effect. They disengaged from each other. She smoothed down her dress and he let out a taking-a-breather 'aah'.

'Mind if we join you for a nightcap?'

'Please do,' Rory lied.

Talk about rubbing his face in it. Two thirty-somethings, not married, not even long into a relationship — pausing for a breather between the prelude of fine dining and the main event. They were happy to stretch the evening out nevertheless, so long as it involved a bit more drinking. No chatting up was required, sex was in the bag. She settled on the sofa opposite Rory while he busied himself at the drinks sideboard.

'I'm Wanda,' Wanda smiled.

She looked pretty, Rory decided. Naturally light-brown hair to her shoulders, a firm, just above slight, figure. Perhaps it was the glow of someone soon to have sex that absorbed Rory.

'Pleased to meet you Wanda, I'm Rory.'

Her impending sex partner handed her champagne. Dark hair and a white body shirt that failed to hide his work-out triceps. No soon-to-have-sex glow — just an un-erasable grin.

'I'm Brett,' he said offering a handshake before sitting down next to Wanda.

'Hi. You two from Melbourne?'

'Yeah. It's the second time we've stayed here. We made a weekend of it a while ago when the Archibald

Exhibition was on at the gallery. We love the place, especially The Manse. Don't we?'

He and Wanda exchanged their best wicked smiles and clinked glasses.

'What about you Rory, are you travelling?' Wanda asked.

'I'm here on work.'

'What do you do?'

'I'm a police detective investigating a murder. What do you two do for a crust?'

It was a bit blunt and cruel but *fuck it*, thought Rory. They needed to be cooled down.

'Err, I work in a furniture showroom in Richmond. Brett is a marina manager,' she said in a distracted automaton tone.

'Who was murdered?' Brett asked soberly.

'I deal with cold cases. I'm reviewing something that happened fourteen years ago. The good thing about it is the wineries that have since sprung up in the murder neighbourhood. Have you been to the local wineries?' Rory added to reverse the conversation out of its solemnity.

'We plan to go home via Heathcote tomorrow actually. I hear their Shirazes are terrific. Do you know much about the area?'

'I'm learning more every day. If you've got a few bob to spend, '04 was a good year for the region. I bought that Mount Campbell Estate red a few days ago,' he nodded toward the drinks sideboard. 'We haven't tried it yet.'

'We?' Wanda and Brett said in unison.

'Me and Mrs Dobell. Not that we are a "we" though. I bought it as a thankyou gift for Mrs Dobell. I would have been keen to taste it if she opened it while I was staying here. Not that Mrs Dobell is obliged in any way to open it while I'm here.'

He managed to stop before his cheeks self-combusted. Wanda and Brett fought to remain expressionless as they exchanged looks yet again. Rory realised how a year of withdrawal left him unpractised in small talk. *The time would have been better spent in a coma*, he decided.

Only an end chair on the twelve-seater table was free when Rory came to the dining room for breakfast. It was serious business for all except the smiling Wanda and Brett. The wedding-goers appeared to be a couple of generations of the same family. They communicated to each other in occasional murmurs. Their grey-haired patriarch, on Rory's right, introduced himself and added, 'Brett tells me you're a detective.'

Rory saw a few heads turn towards him.

'Someone has to do it,' he answered to the table.

The patriarch's chatty efforts foundered on Rory's obfuscating responses. Rory opted for The Manse "special" cooked breakfast. The wedding-goers dribbled from the table silently. Wanda and Brett gave a fellow-travellers' goodbye to Rory.

Sigrid emerged from the kitchen to pour them both coffees. She sat in the patriarch's chair to watch Rory mop up the yolk with his toast.

'Fancy going for a drive today?' Rory asked as he leant back in his chair to consume, but not savour, what Sigrid passed off as coffee.

'I'm sorry. I can't on a Sunday Rory. The middle of the week is my weekend. A houseful like this ties me up today *and* tomorrow.'

His expression caused her to touch his hand.

'I'm sorry Rory. It doesn't mean I wouldn't like to.'

'Sure.'

The next silence was more gawky.

'I guess I'll just have to keep solving the mystery. No rest for the wicked.'

'That takes on a different meaning when a policeman says it. You could be referring to the culprit you're after. You know? Staying on the case. Not giving him time to take a breather.'

'I'm not that quick or clever. It's just me being the wicked one.'

'As long as you stay wicked,' she flirted.

Rory's look approached a smile — a spell too good to break.

Eleven o'clock Sunday morning. Driving alone to Heathcote.

Fuck, fuck, fuck, fuck! Why did I expect her to want to spend an afternoon with me? Do I even like her or has this happened simply because she's unattached and she talked to me? Then again, she did hold my arm when we walked back to the B&B from the Boundary Hotel. But she'd had a few drinks and I'd let a bit of self-pity slip. What if she's got me pegged as a stray puppy? Fuck, fuck, fuck, fuck.

The Heathcote Visitor Information Centre premises added another architectural style to the town's collection. Zinc alum — the modern descendent of corrugated iron, the material that "made the bush in Australia". Late Sunday morning looked like their weekly peak hour. The stand with winery information held the most interest. National parks brochures were only attracting cursory looks from those waiting for a gap to open in front of the winery pamphlets. Rory did a patient circuit of the room while he waited for the two uniformed staff to finish sending aspiring tasting parties on their way.

'I'm interested in the history of the place,' he told the greying male attendant. 'I've been to the historical society clubrooms. They don't seem to open at the weekend. I rang their number and got a machine. Do you know anyone in town who might be able to help me on a Sunday?'

'I'm not sure which members might be around. What did you want to find out about? Is it family history or about the gold rush or the town itself?'

'I'm particularly interested in the area along the Mount Camel Range — going back to pastoral times.'

'Really? That's not a common area of interest, but that may not be a problem. Marjorie Goodwell could help you. She's not a member of the society but she lives out that way. Her family has been there since settlement. She's been documenting their doings for decades. There's not much she won't be able to tell you about that neck of the woods.'

'Will she mind?'

'I'll give her a call if you like.'

'Thanks.'

Rory heard the attendant announce himself on the phone as Ivan Bold and tell Marjorie Goodwell about Rory's interest in meeting her. He broke off and cupped his hand over the receiver to ask Rory, 'And what's your name sir?'

'Detective Sergeant Rory James.'

'Oh … is it an official visit?'

'More of a general inquiry at this stage.'

'Sorry, Marjorie. It's Detective James from the police. He says it's a general inquiry.'

Ivan listened intently for a couple of minutes before finishing the call.

'Okay, I'll send him out. Thanks, Marjorie.'

"Redcastle Creek" was no surprise to Rory but no less impressive for that. The name was carved into the aging stone-walled gateway that was nowhere in sight of the homestead. The century-plus avenue within, too long to call a driveway, passed a weatherboard shearing shed big enough to garage light aircraft. The nearby row of shearers' quarters was anything but humble. From a distance, only the slightly lifting sheets of corrugated roofing iron alluded to faded glory.

Ahead, palm trees, poplars and a protruding cluster of brick chimneys gave a teasing glimpse of the homestead. No faded glory there. The road terminated amid a lawned expanse where it encircled a dry fountain centrepiece. A deep surrounding veranda overlooked the fountain from a raised knoll upon which the house was built. Its roof ran in a long expanse from the veranda eave to the main ridge that hid features other than the lace ironwork below the spouting. Ornate chimneys and a glassed atrium rose beyond the roof ridge.

Marjorie Goodwell stood waiting for him on the path from the fountain to the main entrance. A woman beyond a certain age, as thin as a broom handle and with grey hair pulled from her face into a loosely held bundle. Blue eyes enhanced her still-handsome features.

'Good afternoon, Detective James, I'm Marjorie Goodwell. Welcome to Redcastle Creek.'

'Good afternoon, Mrs Goodwell. It's *Rory* James.'

'Call me Marjorie.'

'What an amazing home, Marjorie.'

He stood, hands on hips, and looked beyond her to take in the homestead's splendour.

'Thank you, Rory. We are very lucky, I know.'

'I'm sure a lot of successful farming had something to do with it,' he said, trying to mirror her welcoming friendliness.

'Generations' worth. More than enough to fill a respectable family history. Not a glorified family tree but a documented history of their accomplishments since settlement of Redcastle Creek. It's not a published tome, I'm not a card-carrying historian. My interest was entirely driven by a desire to capture the family's exploits for posterity. So much gets lost with each passing member of the family.'

'I suppose.'

'Come in,' she said, turning towards the house. They strolled slowly towards the wide stone steps onto the veranda. 'Ivan tells me that you are a fellow history buff.'

'False pretences I'm afraid. For me, history starts and ends with what years Carlton won the premiership. But I'm reviewing the death of Archie Ballantyne and the more I dig, the further back things go. You're probably aware that the case was never closed.'

'You know, I think James Goodwell played in Carlton's 1908 premiership … on the half forward flank. Don't quote me on that. I can look it up if you like.'

'No …,' he paused to stop himself saying "shit", and added instead, 'No kidding. I'm jealous.'

'He was a prodigal son who left the farm. Life went downhill for him after his glory days at Carlton. But that's another story. What about Archie's death?'

She stopped at the base of the veranda steps to face him.

'I've had a few ancient connections pop up. I was hoping your knowledge might extend beyond the front gate. Help me put these things into context.'

'The story of Redcastle Creek goes well beyond the front gate, I can assure you. I have to admit that despite what I just told you, I have been bitten by the history bug. I couldn't stop delving into the district's past after I finished writing "Redcastle Creek – the Grass Grange of Goodwell". I'm actually a Brodie who married into the Goodwell dynasty.

'I've begun doing a book about the independent women who played a part in the settlement of this area.'

She told him about Margaret Hyde, a widow who purchased Mount Campbell Station when it first began. And Jane Hamilton who ran Calbinibin Creek and opened Mount Campbell Inn. She then began rattling off others who operated hotels in the neighbourhood. Like Annie Mitchell Moses at the Black Swan, Clara Judd with Mount Camel Inn and Sarah Voy at the Junction Hotel.

'I was thinking of calling it "The Ladies of Lady's Pass" but that may be confusing now that the winery has adopted the name, Lady's Pass.'

'That's probably not unconnected with what I'm interested in,' Rory said, mustering eagerness.

'Good!' Marjorie said with a smile. 'Well let me get you some tea and you can fire away.'

Marjorie led him to a white-painted wicker table and chairs on the veranda that was already set for tea. The setting was something his grandmother would only have dreamt of owning.

'I'll just go and make a pot.'

Rory sat and waited. He had time to admire the red brick façade of bay windows, each topped with a leadlight design. The raised position of the homestead gave a tree-filtered view to the Mount Camel range and its speckled rectangles of vineyards. Marjorie returned with a tray bearing a china teapot that matched the table's cups and saucers. The biscuits were from a packet.

'I could have baked if I knew you were coming,' she offered.

'We don't always get offered a cup of tea in this job.'

She smiled expectantly as she poured.

'Right. As I said, I'm reviewing Archie Ballantyne's death. Not because anything has come up. It's part of a group of cases being looked at by the Cold Case Unit.'

'So you don't know anything?'

She paused midway through stirring sugar in her tea to lift her knowing eyes to him.

'It's early days,' Rory said, determinedly directing all his attention to his own stirring. The cold-case spiel continued to roll off his tongue. 'But a fresh set of eyes and some modern techniques can reveal a different picture to what investigators faced first time round.'

He placed his teaspoon on the saucer and finally met her gaze. For the shortest of moments, he tried to read her serene face. She took it as a cue.

'What would you like to know about Archie?'

A further nano-pause passed before he began.

'I presume you knew him.'

'Oh yes. At the time, his family and our family were the only descendants of original squatters in the district. Now it's just us.'

'And you know Patrick Seabridge's story about the vineyard that Marcel Chabanne's ancestor established on Archie's ancestors' land?'

'Indeed yes. There's no doubt there was a vineyard up there. The vines might have gone but the winery cellar he built in the hillside on the vine-block is as good as the day it was made. Have you seen it?'

'Yes. Most impressive. It begged the question, why would Antoine Chabanne make such a substantial investment on land he didn't own?'

'That is a sixty-four-thousand-dollar question, Rory. It's hard to know where to start.'

Marjorie readied herself to start nevertheless. She leant back in her chair, held her saucer in one hand and sipped from her cup in the other hand.

'How so?'

'You're talking about a time when ownership of land around here was only just starting to happen. The Government was still writing the rule book and all sorts of politics and questionable practices were at play.

'Victoria had only been occupied by Europeans for about a dozen years before the gold was discovered in 1851. It had a small population and squatters held licences for holdings bigger than English counties. Until then, there was no pressure from anyone wanting to acquire land around here.

'The demand to "unlock the lands" followed the population explosion of the gold rush and I'm afraid to say, my ancestors belonged to the mob that didn't play fair. When the government forbade selecting more than one block a year, squatters used dummies to select land on their behalf — usually other family members and staff. Squatters even had a political slush fund and a corrupt influence over staff in the lands offices. I'm not proud to say our number included more than a few without scruples, Rory.'

She took another sip and placed her cup and saucer on the table.

Rory turned to the distant vines on the slopes of Mount Camel range and asked, 'So what do you think happened with the land Antoine Chabanne was using?'

Marjorie followed his eye across country.

'Most likely he planted his vines under a sub-lease arrangement with Archie's forebears. From what I read at Lady's Pass Run, he had cuttings in potato peel and would have been under pressure to get them in the ground pronto. He wouldn't have had any greater expectations at that stage.'

'But things must have changed by the time he built the cellar and winery.'

'Almost certainly. The land would have passed from pastoral lease to private ownership by then.'

'Do you know to whom?'

'Presumably to Archie's family, although it could have originally been in another name if it had been dummied. You would have to check with the titles office to be sure.'

'But even that might not be accurate if something corrupt happened,' Rory said.

'Exactly.'

Marjorie smiled ruefully.

'Sorry, I'm probably not being much help.'

'You're making things more complicated. But at least I can check it out.'

'It's fascinating to dig around. You'll have the history bug too before you're finished.'

'I hope there's a cure then,' Rory joked, and asked, 'What about the coaching house land? I presume Antoine Chabanne owned that?'

Marjorie broke into a self-satisfied smile.

'How fortuitous that you ask me that. I recently found out that he never owned it at all. It's another part of Seabridge's French story that holds up. When Antoine arrived in Victoria he was not a British subject and was not able to own land. The coaching house was held in the name of Brigid O'Connell, his "partner" in today's parlance. I know this because I researched Brigid for the book I'm doing on Ladies of Lady's Pass. She ran the coaching inn successfully for many years after Antoine was killed.'

'Killed? How?'

Rory's antennae shot up despite the century and a half gap.

'I remember reading that his neck was broken in a fall.'

'Really. Would you be able to find the details?'

'I can try. Why does that interest you?'

'Curiosity more than anything. That's how Marcel died. His neck was broken too.'

'Oh dear. What a cruel coincidence. Remy and Scarlet must be even more devastated to know that.'

'Are they Marcel's Parents?'

'Yes. I've met with them a couple of times lately to find out about Brigid.'

'And do they know much about those times?'

'Yes, as it happens. They made contact with some of Antoine's French descendants when they travelled to France. The family still had heaps of letters that Antoine sent to his family. He was very prolific. They took photocopies and had some of them translated when they returned to Australia.'

'Hmm.'

'Have I given you too much to think about Rory?'

'A bit of homework. Do you have a spare copy of your book I can read?'

Chapter 12

His abiding addiction of the unwelcome sabbatical — the whiff off a double-shot long-black crema as the thick porcelain cup reached his lips. It saved him from cigarettes and from solitary confinement. The compulsory daily walk to Bean Noir Café took him a few shops into the retail strip, amid people with lives. It exposed him to sunlight and was the reason he sometimes washed his clothes. "Double shot long black," were the first words he uttered on any given day, and often the only words. In the end, it was just a nod to Andrew for his usual.

Those memories returned as he sat in Bendigo's Café Essence watching people queue for their requisite cardboard mug to carry into the office. Maybe it also held *them* together, he wondered.

Nadia Kirk arrived.

'Thanks for coming.'

'This better not be an excuse to talk about Lauren.'

Nadia was Lauren James's only remaining Bendigo friend from the time she and Rory lived there. In those days she was Nadia Orlov. Nadia and Lauren's closeness waned with distance and time — until their synchronized separations of a year ago. The ties that bind were suddenly tighter than ever.

For Rory, the degree of difficulty was quadrupled by Nadia's likeness to Lauren. They were sometimes taken to be sisters. The same soft brown eyes gazed at Rory from the familiar, rounded face. The café she chose was across town from her day-job at the Bendigo Bank head office. He chose the footpath table.

'It's strictly work and you're the last person I'd ask unless I had to. Nothing personal Nadia. I've always really liked you.'

'Are you insulting me or hitting on me?'

She smiled at Rory.

'Sorry. Just trying to say this is as awkward for me as it is for you.'

'I can't imagine how I can help you anyway.'

'It's about a body in the morgue.'

'So you said. But I'm the relieving mortuary technician. I only do them when Morgan is away or sick. If it's any other body, I won't have a clue. Shouldn't you be talking to the pathologist?'

'I can't. It's not my case.'

'Even if I did know something, it's not my job to tell you.'

Rory ignored her argument. 'It's about Marcel Chabanne — the bloke who supposedly fell out of a tree near Heathcote.'

'What do you mean, "supposedly"?'

'Well, that's the thing. I happened to be at the scene —
as an observer. I wasn't able to proffer an opinion but I
gathered some pretty serious doubts.'

'I did that one myself. Morgan was away last week.
Broken neck, wasn't it?'

'*You* did it? That's great.'

Her eyes narrowed cynically at him.

'I read the police report. It's one of Cockburn's, isn't
it?'

Rory nodded.

'So that's why you had to keep quiet. You know it was
Cockburn that told Lauren about you and that female
copper? You *are* deep in enemy territory, aren't you?'

Nadia leant back in her chair with savouring-the-
moment smugness.

'I'll let you relish my dilemma for a bit if you like,'
Rory said.

'Lauren should be here for that. I just wish I could have
a moment like this with Jake. He deserves it more than
you.'

'I won't ask you how he is, then.'

'He can never be too miserable as far as I'm
concerned.'

'About Marcel Chabanne,' Rory reminded her.

'It looked straightforward to me. I'm no pathologist
but the broken neck looked consistent with a fall. From a
fair height by the look of the head wound. He must have
lost a fair bit of blood.'

'That's another thing. There was bugger-all blood on the ground and no traces of anyone climbing the tree. Cockburn assumed he fell out of the tree because he was an egg collector. He was found below a magpie nest.'

'So Cockburn didn't treat it as a crime scene?'

'No. If he did, the body would have gone straight to the institute in Melbourne. You and I wouldn't be sitting here now.'

'How sure are you?'

'I've got photos. They show the absence of blood.'

'So what you're saying is — he fell or was pushed from somewhere else high — and then someone placed his body below a bird nest to make it look like he accidently fell from the tree.'

'How else can it be explained?'

'You have to tell Cockburn. The toxicology is due back in a few days. Then it will get signed off as an accident. You're not going to let that happen, are you?'

Her eyes narrowed again.

'Don't look at me like that. Of course I'm gonna tell him. I just needed to make sure first.'

'I suppose.'

'Do you still have his clothes?'

'We usually toss them out unless we have word that the family want them. They might still be in the rubbish skip. I'll be there in the morning if you want me to check.'

'If you could. Can you let me know?'

'Okay then,' she said before adding thoughtfully, 'When this thing becomes an investigation, Cockburn and his mates will soon work out where you came by this info.'

'I won't mention your name.'

'You won't have to, but I don't mind. Cockburn is an arsehole. I'll be telling Lauren about this catch-up too.'

'And she'll tell Cockburn and then he'll be left in no doubt.'

Nadia looked along Bull Street and pensively rolled her tongue in her cheek.

'Perhaps I won't mention it.'

'Beats me why you do that mortuary stuff anyway,' Rory said. 'You don't even get paid.'

'*You* see plenty of dead bodies too. You know how it is. They're just a shell when life has been removed — no longer a person. It's like embroidery for me. I can happily spend a morning taking them apart and stitching them back together. Patching up an accident-mutilated corpse to look like new is peaceful for me. Concealed stitching on the face, the works. I'm proud of the finished product that families see. But if I had to take the life out of one like you did … no way on earth could I do that.'

'You would if you had to … if you didn't have the luxury of thinking about it like this. The hard bit comes afterwards.'

'It's added a few more lines to your face.'

'Nothing the shaver can't deal with,' he said, raking a hand across his cheek and chin.

'Makes you look wiser.'

'You're not travelling too bad yourself.'

'Huh,' she smirked.

'Huh,' Rory smirked back. Not mutual admiration. Mutual empathy for a fellow separate-ee cast unwillingly into the sea of mid-life singledom. They finished coffee with little more to say to each other. Rory stayed seated and watched her walk away. She even walked like Lauren.

Killing someone. How was he ever going to escape reminders while he worked in Homicide? What's a good occupation for forgetting your past? A professional hypnotist's subject? How well does that pay?

'Detective Sergeant Cockburn.' Cockburn's sneer transcended the mobile phone signal.

'Rory James. I need to meet. Where are you?'

'Yeah. What about?'

'Marcel Chabanne.'

'I told you to keep your fucking nose out of that.'

'Do you want to avoid embarrassing yourself with the coroner?'

Without pause, Cockburn answered, 'Where the fuck are you?'

'In Bendigo.'

'Rosalind Park. Ten minutes.'

Rory hit the red button on his mobile, placed the takeaway coffee lid on the Rosalind Park bench space beside himself, took a first sip and waited.

* * *

Rory laced his fingers behind his head as he sat and watched Cockburn arrive. Cockburn's resigned saunter told Rory he had worked it out. He came to a halt and cocked his head with a contemplative look away.

'You're going to tell me it wasn't an accident.'

He turned back to Rory to watch him respond.

'Thought you should know before you sent your paper work off.'

'And just how is it not an accident?'

'No one climbed that tree for a start. You can't lean on an ironbark without leaving a dent. And there were no bike wheel marks in any of the track's soft soil between where the body was found and the highway, although it's possible they were obliterated by Seabridge and us driving in and out.'

'Is that it, nature boy?'

'The body was also found directly below the nest.'

'Duuurrr. Isn't that where it's supposed to land?'

'The branches around the nest were too fine. Even a slight person like Marcel couldn't get close enough to peer into the nest. At best, he would have reached in with an outstretched arm. If he fell at full tilt, his body would have landed a metre nearer to the trunk. I can give you photos.'

'He fell out of a tree. He could have swung … desperately gripping a limb.'

'His head injury. The pathologists say it probably bled a good amount. There was bugger all blood on the ground where he was found. I've got more photos.'

'You spoke to the pathologist?'

'Not directly. You didn't want me to interfere, remember.'

'And this is how you don't interfere, is it?'

'You may be able to retrieve his clothes from the rubbish skip at the Bendigo morgue. I reckon the last thing they'll find is any trace of ironbark.'

'You're joking. How fucking admissible do you think clothes dragged out of a skip would be as evidence? It would only make this cock-up look worse.'

'Please yourself.'

'Oh, for fuck's sake,'

Rory stayed seated on the park bench. Cockburn searched the ground around him for something to kick. He settled for an unsatisfying scuff at the grass with his right foot. 'You knew all this on the day he was found. This isn't about you finding out who killed Chabanne. You kept this to yourself so you could hang me out to dry.'

'Do you think I'd be telling you all this if I wanted to hang you out to dry?'

'Well, what's your fucking story. Why tell me now?'

'Despite what you think, I'm a detective. Do you expect me to do nothing when I come across a dumped body? I wanted to be sure. You weren't in the mood for listening or countenancing any doubt, you might recall.'

Cockburn glimpsed the resolve in Rory's dark eyes. He knew it was no olive branch.

'So that's it? You tell me. I go off and find out who did it and you go back to your cold case.'

'Have you found out who wanted to buy Chabanne's house?'

'I've got someone chasing it up. It wasn't a priority, as things stood.'

'And you'll let me know what they find out?'

'What's it to you? You said you only wanted to know if Seabridge was involved.'

'I've changed my mind. I want to know the whole story — who's in, who's out. Look ...' he took an emphasising pause, 'The stuff I've just told you is not insignificant. Have you got a problem letting *me* know stuff?'

'Okay. I'll let you fucking know.'

'I also want to speak to Chabanne's parents about the cold case.'

'You're not telling me the cases are connected again, are you?'

'Not that I know of, but the Chabannes and the Ballantynes were neighbours for a hundred and fifty years. The Chabannes and Seabridge for fourteen years.'

'You can get their details from Logan. Give me time to let the Chabannes know we're treating their son's death as suspicious.'

'I'll be calling in to see them tomorrow on my way back to Melbourne.'

Rory watched Cockburn pace against the backdrop of Bendigo's historic streetscape.

'You think I've got something on you now. Something I can use,' he said to Cockburn.

'You wouldn't want to try.'

'You're right. I wouldn't. But not because of you. Not everyone is like you.'

'I hope you're not expecting gratitude. As far as I'm concerned, you're just doing what a good copper should have done.'

'Even when you didn't?'

Chapter 13

'I had to start without you.' Sigrid Dobell's voice floated from the parlour of The Manse.

Rory closed the heavy front door behind him and peered into the lamp-lit chamber. He slid the laptop carry case from his shoulder and entered.

'Cleared your weekend workload then?'

'Yes. Just you and me tonight. You can have the four-poster back if you like.'

'I wouldn't mind, but it's hardly worth moving. I have to head back to Melbourne tomorrow.'

'Oh.'

Rory shrugged, trying not to look flattered at her disappointed tone.

'Have you solved the case?'

'If only it were that easy.'

'Just thought I'd ask. What's the official line?'

'Progress is being made. There are promising lines of inquiry. Choose your own cliché. What we haven't got is someone helping us with our inquiries.'

'Well if I can't offer you a celebratory drink, how about one to drown your sorrows?'

'Best offer I've had all day.'

Sigrid rose to pour him a scotch. Her bare feet made the moment somehow intimate.

'If it's your last night, how about we go out for a meal again — make up for me being tied down over the weekend.'

'To our usual?'

'Do we have a usual after one visit?'

'We will if we go there again tonight.'

Their "usual" table. Small talk came easier and their respective pasts were cautiously revealed, albeit to Curriculum Vitae shallowness — both deflected true intimacy with the dexterity of a Bob Dylan interview. He was separated, has two children he doesn't see enough of, and had taken a year off work after being involved in a shooting. Yes, he was the hero policeman who shot the man attacking a policewoman with a knife. No, he was no hero. Yes, he was pleased to be back on the job.

Of her most recent divorce, 'We drifted apart.'

Flirting crept in. 'So it's been a while since either of us drank from the well.'

She held his arm with relaxed nonchalance on their stroll back to The Manse. It took a moment for her to find the front door key. She hesitated to turn it in the lock, taking advantage of the dark to tell him, 'This horse you're trying to get back on, perhaps some additional therapy might be in order.'

She moved towards him but was balked as his body stiffened to a statue beneath her touch. Once again, he felt the unveiling silk slide to the floor. His mind flew ahead to naked after-sex sleeping — lying beside her when he awoke in a blathering sweat-drenched panic.

The nightly nightmare had returned since his encounter with Cockburn. Always the same dream. The knife assailant lunging not at Heidi, but at Lauren, Nick and Steph. Rory shooting at him and watching the bullets pass the assailant's raging face in cartoon-like slow motion. Rory unable to kill the knife wielder and unable to stop the attack. The therapist told him it indicated feelings of guilt for the victim's family. Surely for his own family, Rory contended. Surely he was a victim too — a victim of post-shooting trauma.

It took months for the nightmare's frequency to wane as the therapist took him through admitting his problem, grieving and developing a determination to change. Determination to change had not deserted him, nor had the flashbacks returned. But the nightmare had reclaimed his nights. Sleeping was not something he could trust himself to share.

Sigrid watched him with wounded stupefaction.

'Would you hold it against me if I say no?' Rory said lamely.

'I could give you a flirty answer if you hadn't killed the moment.'

'It's not that I don't want to …'

She silenced him with a finger on his lips.

'It's okay. I don't need to know. Maybe you could come and stay when you're not working.'

Chapter 14

There was no blue Golf when Rory arrived at the coaching house.

Rory stayed in the car while he phoned Bendigo police station and asked Constable Caiden Logan for the Chabannes' phone number.

'Thanks Caiden. Catch you later,' he said with the Chabannes mobiles, land line and Melbourne address now in his notebook.

He tried the land line. Remy Chabanne's voice was even more disheartened than he anticipated from years of dealing with victim's relatives. He assumed Remy had not long learnt from Cockburn that Marcel's death was suspicious — he didn't want to ask.

Rory explained that in the course of another investigation he happened to attend the police response to Marcel's body being found. It was something he needed to speak to Remy and his wife Scarlet about. Remy uttered a supremely uninterested 'oh,' before telling Rory they had returned to Melbourne the previous morning to make funeral arrangements. The service would be held in Melbourne. They could meet him at their Camberwell home the day after the funeral.

It was a call neither could end quickly enough.

Rory stood from his car and reached for the key hidden behind the geranium. It was gone. He tried the front door. It was open.

He paused with the door knob still in hand.

'Anyone there?' he called into the silence.

As his eyes adjusted slowly to the unlit interior, a monstrously distorted version of the discerning décor — one hundred and fifty years in the making — emerged.

'Fuck!'

Rory locked his feet where he stood and swivelled to scan the room. The ransacker's search had been for hidden treasure. Pictures taken from the walls were removed from their frames but not stolen. A search of the chimney had spilt an apron of soot in front of the fireplace. Sooty footprints had been deliberately smudged to conceal tell-tale treads or shoe size. Chair linings were lifted, cushions were opened using the zip, architraves and other fittings were prised from the walls in a quest to examine every cranny.

Rory backed from the room and returned wearing disposable shoe covers and gloves. He moved through the house to discover the same pattern in every room. The search appeared methodical rather than frenzied. Drawers of bird eggs were removed from the collection cabinet but few of the eggs were broken. The cabinet had been moved from its alcove, its rear lining prised enough to peer into the enclosed void. The half-renovated bathroom now matched the décor of the rest of the house.

No room was left unturned. Nor had any of the outbuildings, although a more destructive approach was evident — a sign that frustration at not finding the grail had set in.

Rory flipped open his mobile phone and dialed.

'Detective Sergeant Cockburn.'

'Rory James,' Rory announced. 'You'd better get out to the Chabannes' coaching house with a crime scene crew. The Chabannes have gone back to Melbourne and the place has been ransacked.'

'You're a shit magnet, you know?'

'It's my knack of being in the wrong place at the right time, remember?'

'Don't remind me. What's the story?'

'It's not my case.'

'Don't milk it. Humour me with a guess.'

'It could simply be vultures preying on the dead. I've seen that happen in country towns when an old-timer dies. People expect money to be stashed under the bed. This is more likely to be connected with Marcel's killing though. Whoever did it, pulled the place apart but in a respectful way. Hardly an egg shell broken.'

'Someone was after something?'

'Yeah. But my guess is they left empty-handed.'

* * *

After a week on the job, the sum of Rory's inwards correspondence was a post-it note stuck to his computer monitor telling him to see Detective Inspector Richard Bourke as soon as he was back in the office. The Archie Ballantyne file lay closed on his desk and several other bound cold-case files sat unattended in his in-tray.

Rory peered at the assortment of workstations beyond the glass office-front. None of the names was familiar but a few of the faces had been passing Rory in the foyer for years. His new workspace neighbours were mainly public servants with the Commercial and Electronic Branch. There was no space on the Homicide floor for its Cold Case Unit. Even the clean desk fanatics among his co-floor-occupants had a family photo, holiday snapshot or ludicrous cartoon figure atop their PC monitor. Rory peered around his sterile office cubicle and made a mental note to buy some sort of adornment, picture calendar or knick-knack — anything.

He climbed the stairwell to the Homicide floor and strode through the mostly empty open office plan to Bourke's office. The faces of the only two workstation occupants were not familiar to Rory from a year ago. Rory's anonymity and a smile from Fran, Bourke's long time PA, calmed him.

'Come in, Rory,' Bourke offered without taking his thick fingers from the keyboard. 'I'll just get this email away.'

Rory sat opposite and watched Bourke's frown spread to his bald crown, then suddenly un-crease as he clicked the send button and lifted his head to smile at Rory.

'How was your first week back?' he asked.

'It'd be a lot more normal if you stopped being so nice to me,' he joked.

'Okay. If you want the bad cop. How about an occasional phone call or email? That would be nice for starters. I'm hearing about what you're up to from others. Do you think that makes me look good? And what do I hear? You're tangling with Cockburn. I managed to shift him off the scene for your return and who is the first person you go and see? Jesus fucking Christ, Rory.'

'It wasn't planned.'

'Even fucking so, you should have just walked away and left him to it. If Cockburn fucks things up in the sticks, then let him.'

Rory went into a tight-lipped shutdown.

'Look Rory. A lot of cops would kill to have the job you've been given. But I don't want some lazy bastard swanning around the countryside drinking lattes and regurgitating what we did first time round. I want someone who can take a fresh look and figure out who is responsible for the murders. If there's not enough evidence to follow through, then I want something I can at least leak to the media. Let crooks know they can run but they can't hide. Let the public know we don't give up.'

He held his cheeks for a moment In search of something more convincing.

'It might seem like light-duty therapy to you but that doesn't make it any less important in the scheme of things. You've been off for a year and having therapy for Christ's sake. I need to see you crawl before you start sprinting again. This is my investment in you. If you fuck it up, a disability payout won't be optional. Just get your head down and get on with it. Got it?'

'Yeah,' Rory said repentantly. Citing mitigating circumstances was not permissible. Not wearing them on his stoic face however was impossible. The mental scars had sucked the effortless composure from his dark features.

Bourke rolled his pen backwards and forwards with his fingers on the workstation and studied Rory. The homily-ending silence broke when a computer chime signalled incoming email. Bourke reached for the mouse to see who it was from. 'You wish,' he scoffed to the screen before bringing his attention back to Rory.

'Have you got a problem working on your own?' he asked in a softening tone. Rory unstiffened in his chair.

'I prefer it at this stage,' he answered.

'That's what I thought. But don't turn it into a "me versus the rest of the world thing". Cockburn and Heidi are lost causes. Cockburn wouldn't be treating you differently if the shooting didn't happen. You know what he's like — no head, no arms, no legs — just one big shoulder with a chip on it.'

Rory's eyelids lifted a touch at his boss's frankness. Bourke noticed and paused a beat.

'And Heidi's a victim who needs someone to blame. Everyone else has moved on, whatever you imagine they're thinking. Don't forget you got the public backing of the Commissioner.'

'It's not about Cockburn and Heidi,' Rory lied.

'You're not the only cop who shot someone and you're not the only cop that screwed around and fucked his marriage. If you're not ready to work again then I wanna know. So let me ask you again and give me a straight answer. How was your first week back?'

Rory didn't hesitate to grab the clean slate he was offered. He leant forward receptively.

'Good. Better because of this thing with Cockburn, I think.'

'How so?'

'If it was just the cold case I'd have felt like I was just going through the motions and I'd be none the wiser about how I was doing. With the Cockburn thing, there's a bigger picture emerging, even if the cases don't end up being connected. It got my juices flowing again.'

'Can you work with Cockburn if you need to? It's not heading for another shit fight between you two, is it?

Rory looked into his lap for a moment before lifting a solemn face to answer.

'When I ran into him out of the blue he went for the jugular. I was off guard and to be honest, I thought I wasn't gonna handle it. But the element of surprise soon wore off. I could cope with him if I had to but he doesn't want to deal with me on this and that suits me fine. I'll work with him if I discover a connection between the cases.'

'You mean if he has no choice?'

'I mean if I had no choice.'

'And what are the chances that the deaths are connected?'

'Too early to tell. But the history of the place is so interwoven that if I had to put money on it …'

Chapter 15

Past the classic boutique Hotel Lindrum in Flinders Street, the adjoining un-Melbourne-like stepped pedestrian canyon to Flinders Lane, the copse of elegant trees in a sandy alcove nestled between the footpath and the rising granite-clad Shell House skyscraper. Rory rode its lift to the upper floors of number one Spring Street — no longer Shell House since the oil giant sought anonymity in the suburbs, but a shell nevertheless, its scallop curve anomalous in the city's right-angled filled skyline.

The Department of Regional Development receptionist ushered him to a conference room where he waited for Marina Clarebrough, the Director of Regional Strategy and Initiatives.

The unimpeded city-edge view arced 180 degrees to capture every landmark — Port Phillip Bay and its traffic of container ships, Flinders Street Station, Sidney Myer Music Bowl, the MCG, the tennis centre. Every icon appeared close up, except for the railway yards across the street. They resembled a model train set that someone in the building had a controller for.

'On a clear day you can see Port Phillip Bay heads,' Marina Clarebrough said as she entered and stood shoulder to shoulder with Rory at the window. Rory sensed the cheerful Bakelite-brown brunette of a certain age had never married. Her flouncy hair and flouncy dress attained corporate chic appositeness under a black designer jacket. Rory could no longer picture a Director of Regional Strategy and Initiatives dressing otherwise.

'Impressive,' was all Rory could manage.

'Can I call you Rory?' Marina smiled. 'And can we get you a drink? Tea or coffee?'

Rory had failed to notice that the receptionist had come to the door. Marina chose mineral water and Rory a black coffee. He was pleased to learn it wouldn't be instant.

They sat across a corner of the large meeting table — Marina side on to the window, Rory with the full view. She placed her iPhone on the table.

'You were vague on the phone, which police branch are you with, Rory?' she asked.

'The Homicide Cold Case Unit.'

Her face lit up. 'A cold case murder, how intriguing. I expected something corporate when you mentioned the Lady's Pass Museum of Art project. One of the players getting into financial strife perhaps. Not a murder. Who died? Who did it?'

'I'm reviewing a death that happened on the property about fourteen years ago. At the time, the Coroner gave an opening finding. We still don't know if it was a murder or accidental death.'

'And can you tell me who it was?'

'An old-timer farmer called Archie Ballantyne. He was the previous owner of the property. Patrick Seabridge discovered his body the day the sale was settled.'

'Does that mean Patrick had no reason to kill him?'

'You're getting too far ahead. That's not how we handle an investigation like this.'

'I bow to your expertise, Rory. It simply sprang into my mind,' she said with some animated waving of her hands. 'Patrick Seabridge is the only common link I know of between the Lady's Pass project and what you say happened fourteen years ago.'

'It's a delicate matter,' Rory said too coyly. 'We have to establish if a murder occurred before we begin searching for individuals that might have reason to do so. There are of course many individuals who might have a motive if that were the case.'

Marina's inner brow lowered.

'All right Rory. I work in government too. I understand exactly what you are at pains not to say. Ask me what you like without the police-speak, and I'll keep my inklings to myself.'

Rory drew a long hard breath through his nose and placed his notebook on the table.

'Don't look so glum,' she continued. 'Think of me as one of your own. The Lady's Pass project will involve a lot of public money — your taxes and mine. You probably didn't intend to, but you just added this to my to-do list. If a shadow is being cast we'll need to know well before the shit hits the fan. There's no shortage of ministers to turn the first sod or cut the ribbon. But it's my job to make sure their mugs are not on the front page of *The Age* and the *Herald Sun* in a story about one of our projects going pear-shaped. You might not think it's your problem but, rest assured, it's an imperative that will be made clear to your boss.'

Rory kept his straight bat in play.

'I'm trying to build up a long-term picture before and after Archie Ballantyne's death.'

'Okay, Rory. I'll surrender to your police euphemisms,' she said raising her hands slightly in mock surrender. 'I'll tell you everything I can, provided you agree to give me a heads up the second you uncover anything adverse in relation to the project. If you detect one squinzillionth of a molecule of something that is not quite right, I want to know. You won't have to tell me what it is. I'll just need to know if a runaway Mack truck is heading our way. It's the only chance I'll have of managing the fallout. Do we have a deal?' Marina smiled coldly.

Rory smiled back. 'I can see what makes a good Director of Regional Strategy and Initiatives.'

'I'm glad we understand each other. So what has Mr Seabridge been up to?'

The receptionist chose the moment to bring in a tray with a glass of water for Marina and coffee for Rory. He waited for the receptionist to leave before continuing.

'I wasn't being deliberately vague when I said I'm trying to build up a long-term picture before and after Archie Ballantynes's death. The history of the place before Archie's death gets more intriguing the more I learn. As for what's happened since then, well … Seabridge discovered another "accident" victim last week.'

'Really? And they're connected?'

'There's no obvious link and it's difficult to imagine one with such a long gap between corpses. The latest one's not my case. The investigating officer is assuming they're not connected at this stage.'

'It sounds like you have a different view.'

'I have an open mind. Taking a long-term perspective might shine a different light on things.'

'Who died this time?'

'A reclusive neighbour called Marcel Chabanne.'

'Should I be worried about this having an impact on the project?'

'It's not for me to say, but give me a call if you're about to issue any media releases about the project. I'll tell you if anything has come up in the meantime.'

'Was that a wink, Rory?'

He smiled. 'How about I have a turn at asking questions?'

The smile worked.

'All right. Shoot,' Marina said, straightening to quiz-show contestant attentiveness.

'Tell me about Seabridge.'

Rory took the chance to try his coffee.

'He's an unusual creature. The last thing I want to do is confer undue praise on the bloke but in a way, I liken him to Mick Jagger — someone you'd least expect to have consummate business acumen. And yet, *Sir* Mick, still has as much rock cred as the day the press implored Britain to "lock up your daughters".

'Well, Seabridge also has a happy knack of straddling business and the arts. He's not artistic in any way but his roots are deep in the arty end of Melbourne. His family have been art dealers for decades and Patrick has always played his part in that enterprise. But he also dabbles in managing the odd rock band and had a hand in promoting some of the more successful music festivals. He was a partner in Z restaurant when it first started — before its fall from grace. You'll learn that he has a knack of not being around when things go belly up. But that might be because he's a clever businessman.

'The art people love his rock cred and the music types are impressionable about his art knowledge. He of course plays up to both. If you've met him you will know just how erudite he can appear. People are easily drawn to him.'

'Some of my colleagues have a less polite term for the type.'

She lifted the corner of her mouth to acknowledge his meaning.

'I'm not so cynical because I know he knows his stuff. I'm more concerned about the long-term picture and his ability to follow through. He has a good nose for discovering successful bands but they usually end up switching to mainstream managers once they achieve success. The same thing with music festivals. He seems to lose interest when things become routine. He's more of an ideas man than a doer.

'The reason we're taking the Lady's Pass project seriously is because it's based on art and wine — two dependable mainstays in his life — and the people he plugs into in the art world. Do you want me to drop names?'

'I'm well aware, thanks.'

Rory was pleased to have a chance to infer he had some knowledge about what Seabridge was up to.

'Projects of this size don't come through the front door and Seabridge is not the type to fill in a form. Like I said, the art world is full of the richest names in town and if Seabridge hasn't got them investing directly, then he has persuaded them to at least sit on his art museum advisory board. The Premier himself is Minister for the Arts, you know. So the first we heard about the project was via various ministers.'

Marina's words trailed off as she reached for her phone. It had begun to flash silently. Her promptness in picking it up suggested to Rory that it was a meeting-escape strategy pre-arranged with her PA. If it was, then she had decided she didn't need it. Her thumb dismissed whatever the phone demanded without time to read the screen. Her attention was back on Rory before he could take in the view of Port Phillip Bay again. *This can't be going too bad*, he decided.

'Sorry about that. As I was saying, the first *we* heard about the project was via various ministers. In that sense, it already has approval and our job is to take it through the due diligence motions — knocking their fuzzy business case into order, coordinating input from Tourism Victoria, Arts Victoria, the Planning Department, water authority, infrastructure, you name it. Presenting it to the Major Investment Unit parliamentary committee.'

'Is the project going to fly? I know it's out there, but it seems to have stalled.'

Rory's observation brought a complimenting smile.

'Very astute, Rory. It's been a while since the all-singing all-dancing launch with a Lyons Architecture design, artists and parliamentary representatives.'

She made charleston-dancing hand gestures.

'That's not unusual for these proposals. The razzamatazz is often run early to garner further investment and to have a straw man that will flush out likely opponents. It's also what Seabridge is good at — all zeal and all zeal. But this one has gone on longer than I expected. Their merchant banker told us that the delay is because of a switch in hotel chains. The hotel was originally going to be under the Novamont banner but now they are negotiating with the lesser-known Swiss-based Evard Group — ostensibly because of the Swiss connection with Buvelot.'

Rory flipped open his spiral notebook for the first time during their meeting.

'Is that a first crack? Do you know why Novamont pulled the pin?' he asked.

She squared her iPhone with the table edge before answering.

'I have to admit the thing is stacking up rather well so we didn't see a need to chase down the Novamont withdrawal. I can find out for you if you think it has any relevance.'

No smile from Marina. The offer was made as a challenge to Rory. She didn't appreciate having an intel gap exposed.

'If you could, please,' Rory replied as he made scratchy notes about Novamont and the Evard Group. He found himself thinking, *I should also make a note to get back into the habit of writing more of this stuff down.*

'Anything else I can tell you?' she said to break Rory's reverie.

'Not for now. I get the picture and I don't have a desire to swap jobs with you.'

'Like Mick said, *It's only rock and roll, (but I like it).'*

'Yeah. He also said *You can't always get what you want.'*

'Showing our age aren't we, Rory, or is this a boys' pissing competition?' She laughed before half singing,

'*Bu: if you try some time, you just might find, you get what you need.*'

Rory clapped twice and grinned. 'A singing Director of Regional Strategy and Initiatives. Not what I expected to meet today.'

'It's one of my initiatives. I'll phone you about the Novamont thing.'

'Looking forward to it already.'

Chapter 16

'So this is the Cold Case cubby then?'

Rory looked up from his computer to see Cockburn draped in the door jamb of his office.

'What are you doing here?'

'Don't worry. I'm only passing through. I'm stuck in Bendigo for another month yet. Bourke told me to pop down and see you.'

'Yeah? What about?'

'Who are your wanker mates?' Cockburn said cocking his head to the grid of workstations beyond Rory's office door. 'Commercial and Elec-fucking-tronic Branch. It must be a laugh a minute down here.'

'It's who's not here that counts.'

Cockburn gave his stiff version of a wry grin and sat in the only visitor chair.

'Sopwith Camels? Since when have you been into old planes?'

Rory cringed. It was the wrong time of year to buy a calendar — his sole personalised addition to the office. At this time of year, the only choice was bi-planes or David Beckham.

'Did you only come here to hang shit?'

'The approach the Chabannes had to buy the coaching house. Turns out it was from the Habdouds. We've come down to Melbourne to bring them in for questioning.'

'Is that name meant to mean something to me?'

'I forgot you've been under a rock for the past twelve months. Habdoud is the Lebanese family with no visible means for their considerable wealth. The mob who are having a very public feud with their gang rivals. They have a riverside holiday McMansion at Echuca and regularly pass the coaching house along the way.'

'And why do they want to get hold of the coaching house?'

'That's what we're down here to find out. Maybe they want to go legit and open a doner kebab takeaway.' The sneer broke into a smile at his own humour.

'You're enjoying this, aren't you?'

'It'll be like the Armed Offenders Squad days. Dealing with real crims. These families have no qualms about bumping each other off. A recluse in the bush? Like swatting a mosquito for this mob.'

'They don't sound like the type to fake a bird nest egg collecting accident.'

Rory's mobile rang.

'Steph? What's up?'

The body language of someone hearing bad news put the Cockburn sneer on pause.

'Oh, Steph.'

The static of a faintly amplified voice continued for too long. Cockburn fidgeted.

Another 'Oh, Steph …'

'She was …'

'… She was.'

'… I don't know if I should, Steph,' he sighed heavily.

The gravity of the conversation seemed to rise even higher. He dropped his eyes and listened with sombre stillness. A minute or two passed until he uttered 'Uh huh … uh huh.'

As the caller continued to speak, Rory began nodding with a response poised on his lips.

'I'll be there. Just let me know when.'

He lifted his eyes to see Cockburn with his arms crossed. He looked back down.

'Okay.

'And Steph … I love you.'

Cockburn watched Rory stare at his mobile phone to absorb the news.

'Lauren's mother Beryl died this morning,' Rory finally offered.

'Your ex fucking wife's mother?'

'If you must.'

The Chabanne's Melbourne home was predictably Camberwell-ian. Leafy Broadway was more like a bitumenised grove than a street. The Chabanne's slate roof Victorian stood out as one of its earlier residences among the imposing Californian bungalows. Along the way, one of its owners, perhaps the Chabannes, had bridged the size gap with a two storey in-character extension at its rear.

Scarlet Chabanne had agreed to see Rory while Remy was at work. The woman who greeted Rory had unfussy grey hair but none of the lines that come with corresponding age. Marcel Chabanne's mother reflected her son's slight height and fine build.

'Thank you for seeing me so soon after the funeral,' Rory offered as she led him down a hallway with an arch midway along its length. Rory glimpsed various living rooms opening off the original Victorian section. At the hallway end, colour-trimmed architraves gave way to an expansive living area lit with down lights and large timber-framed windows. The contrasting modern décor was nevertheless timeless in style.

They sat on two-seater sofas positioned either side of a pale timber coffee table. Scarlet faced Rory against a leafy garden backdrop that defied the existence of any neighbours. Tea was served with a selection of small slices. From a Burke Road artisan bakery, Rory surmised.

'So you're not actually dealing with Marcel's death?'

'I'm afraid not, Mrs Chabanne. I happened to be visiting Lady's Pass Run about this other matter when Marcel was found. I'm sorry about your loss.'

'Thank you,' Scarlet said, lifting her cup and saucer to take a sip.

Rory paused from his own two-handed sip. 'I'm with the Cold Case Unit. I'm reviewing Archie Ballantyne's death. I presume you knew Archie?'

'Yes indeed. Archie kept an eye on the coaching house for us and made a point of calling in whenever we stayed there. We followed the case very closely at the time.'

'You and your husband?'

'Yes. Remy and I both attended the inquest.'

'Then you'll know how it was left unresolved.'

'Is there new information about Archie's death?'

'This review is purely as a consequence of the Cold Case Unit being set up. It's up to me to unearth any new information.'

'So what are your chances? There was so little to go on originally, surely that dearth can only have lessened in the meantime.'

'You never know with a cold case approach. Things sometimes emerge that were overlooked for whatever reason. Emotions of the day distract from mundane but nevertheless significant matters. A pattern can also form when the future is added to the past, as it were.'

'Even so, I can't see how our infrequent presence at Lady's Pass can shed light on the matter. We were travelling in Europe when it happened. It was before Marcel's accident. He spent less time there than us in those days. At the time, we knew too little for the police to take a statement from us.'

'I'm constructing a long-term picture of Archie's property and from what I have gathered so far, Remy's great-great-grandfather had a substantial involvement in it for his vines and winemaking.'

'You would have discovered that from the letter that Patrick Seabridge has hanging on the wall at Lady's Pass Run.'

'Exactly. I've also spoken with Marjorie Goodwell from Redcastle Creek.'

'I can confirm that Antoine Chabanne leased part of the land 150 years ago if that's what you want to know. But from what we can gather, the family relinquished its interest when Antoine died at a relatively young age. As I understand it, he had use of the place for less than twelve years. The vines probably withered without him, or died of phylloxera.'

'Does your husband have greater knowledge of the family history — being a Chabanne descendant?'

She tilted her head to peer upwards with a slightly scornful frown.

'I suppose there was no tactful way for you to ask that, Detective James. But don't be concerned, you *are* talking to the right person. Remy and I were both stimulated by the Claude Gatineau letter that Patrick Seabridge uncovered. In the end, it was *I* who dug deeper into the family connections.'

'What did you find out?'

'It wasn't easy to find anything much at first. Antoine Chabanne set out as a vanguard to find a new life for him and his many siblings. That never eventuated because he died and his Irish wife Brigid didn't have French writing skills to stay in touch with Antoine's family. In fact, I discovered that she and Antoine never married. Their son, however, did bear the Chabanne name. The coaching house land was bought in Brigid's name O'Connell because Antoine was not able to own land as a non-British subject. Her name is still on the title.'

'Marjorie Goodwell told me that you visited Antoine's family in France. Were you able to fill in any blanks then?'

'Some of them. It wasn't too hard to track down the Chabanne family. They still live in Condrieu. They were so excited to discover that Antoine had living descendants continuing the Chabanne name in Australia. It was difficult though after the first euphoric phone call and emails. These were the days before *Skype* was around and, in any case, we didn't speak much French and none of them spoke much English. That's when we decided to travel to France and visit them. Marcel and his brother Andre came. It was such an exciting trip.'

The memory had distracted her into a smile.

'We didn't need language to share each other's joy. Especially having Marcel and Andre there. Our tourist French got us by and added to the fun. Funnily enough, the Australian Chabannes had always chosen French Christian names. It went down so well. We were all discovering relatives we didn't know we had. Can you imagine?'

'I'm envious thinking about it,' Rory said — *envious of anyone else's family these days.*

The oral history of Antoine was alive and well within his French family. Antoine had been a prolific letter writer and most of them were preserved in an old trunk. They talked about him as if they knew him personally. We understood their enthusiasm but we all knew the details were falling on deaf ears. While we were there, they photocopied all of Antoine's letters and we still have copies. Our neighbour Cate teaches French and she was kind enough to begin translating them for us.'

'Didn't she finish the job?'

'She was elderly and died after finishing only a few. I'm afraid we didn't have another such convenient means to translate the rest. By that stage we already had a flavour of Antoine's life and it became less of a priority. We have never bothered to have the rest done.'

'In the letters that *were* translated, was there anything about the land arrangements?'

'I think there was, but nothing that I remember as significant.'

'Do you mind if I have a look at them? I'm happy to make copies and have them destroyed later. I might even be able to have some more translation done. I also have a neighbour who knows French.'

'It sounds all right. I'll check with Remy though, if you don't mind.'

Scarlet held her fingers to the side of her chin with the worry of a thought she wanted to express.

'Is something else bothering you, Mrs Chabanne?' Rory asked.

The animation of the family reunion memory had disappeared. She eventually answered in a much weaker voice. 'Have you considered that Marcel's death may be connected somehow?'

'Do you have some reason to think that Mrs Chabanne?'

'Nothing in particular, but it made me shudder when I heard that Marcel was found by Patrick Seabridge. I couldn't look at him at the funeral.'

'It's not my case Mrs Chabanne. You'll need to speak to Detective Sergeant Cockburn about that.'

'I thought you might say that,' she said, sounding greatly disappointed.

'If I do come across anything, it won't be ignored.'

'Thank you.'

The barely audible reply told Rory it was not enough.

He pressed the green button of his mobile phone and answered, 'Detective Sergeant James.'

'*Pleased to meet you, hope you guess my name, but what's puzzling you, is the nature of my game,*' a female voice answered.

'The Stone's *Sympathy for the Devil,* bonus points,' Rory answered cheerfully.

'Thought you'd be impressed. I had to make up for drawing a blank on why Novamont pulled out of the project,' Marina Clarebrough told Rory.

'That's a shame.'

'It's strictly commercial in confidence as far as they're concerned — no question. They wouldn't divulge their thinking to the Lady's Pass Museum of Art consortium and they certainly wouldn't be telling a third party like us.'

'Did you tell them the police are asking?'

'You'd have a hard time convincing them how it's relevant.'

'So *It's all over now?*'

'Classic '60s Rolling Stones. Very good, Detective.' He imagined her smiling, 'I thought I might have had some luck with one of the consultants who worked on the business case assessment for us. He's done some work for Novamont in the past. He had a vague memory of hearing about a problem with the land. But I checked it out and drew another blank. Our team had already commissioned a title search and found no ownership issues. No tricky covenants, no outstanding mortgages. Sorry.'

'Not your fault. I appreciate your trying.'

'No problem. Don't forget our understanding. If this starts heading south …'

'What? No Rolling Stone sign-off?'

'It's getting too hard. I had to Google the last one.'

'Time for a new game,' Rory said without thought.

The phone went quiet.

'Are you still there?' he asked.

'Yeah. I was trying to decide if I should read anything into your flirting.'

'Only if you want to,' he heard himself answer before they both made hasty goodbyes.

Christ, thought Rory. *The second time in a week. Why did this never happen to me when I was eighteen?* And when it did happen, there was ironic unrequitedness at play. Like the perpetual frustration of an overly strung-out sit-com plot.

Chapter 17

It was after eleven in the morning before Cockburn got the word that brothers Eugene and Stephen Habdoud had driven from the family's Centenary Avenue home in the Melbourne suburb of Moreland. The house would now be occupied by patriarch, Mansur Habdoud, his wife Rashida and daughter Nina. Cockburn drove into the street and parked with a long view to the high rendered brick fence that fronted the property. The long morning wait had exhausted police gossip and the Carlton-Essendon game post-mortem with his passengers — Sergeant Bill Bolton of the Crime Gangs Taskforce and Sergeant Millar O'Callaghan of the Special Operations Group. Minds were now on the job as they waited for word that the Habdoud brothers were detained in Bell Street for a suspected unroadworthy vehicle check. When the call came by police radio, O'Callaghan gave the word: 'Go.'

A mini bus of six SOG members came Into the street and parked opposite the electronically operated garage entrance. Marked cars blocked the street at each end and

Cockburn drove the short distance to park kerbside at the front gate.

He and Bolton alighted and strode to the intercom in flak jackets. Cockburn was surprised to hear a voice emerge from the speaker grille before he reached for the button.

'What?'

'Am I speaking to Mansur Habdoud?' Cockburn asked.

'Don't you pricks *know* whose door you're knocking on?'

'I'm Detective Sergeant Cockburn of the Bendigo CIU. We have cause to believe you can assist us in our enquiries about a death we're investigating. We'd like to ask you some questions please.'

'What death in Bendigo? I don't know anything about no death. I wanna talk to my sons first.'

Cockburn and Bolton heard Mansur Habdoud and a woman begin an animated conversation in Lebanese Arabic.

'Mr Habdoud. Mr Habdoud.' Cockburn yelled into the intercom. The background argument ceased and Cockburn continued. 'Can you please open the gate so I can explain the situation to you.'

'You want me to let you in so you can drag me away and pin some murder on me? No fucking way. I wanna talk to my sons about what murder you're talking about.'

'We're not here to take you into custody, Mr Habdoud. We are only asking you to come to the police station to answer some questions.'

'You're not arresting me? Bull-fucking-shit. How come you're wearing armour if you only want me to answer fucking questions?'

'We're wearing flak jackets because your sons are suspected of carrying firearms. In fact they are now known to carry a pistol. They were found with a pistol in your car when they were stopped by police a few minutes ago. Now we also need your version of why there is a pistol in your car.'

'I wanna see Eugene.'

'You can see Eugene all you want, after you answer our questions.'

'I wanna lawyer.'

'Phone your lawyer now. Can you open the gate please, Mr Habdoud?'

The Lebanese argument erupted again in the background. Bolton looked to Cockburn to see how he would proceed.

'All of this crap and now the pistol thing — we only want to question the prick,' Cockburn said to Bolton without concern that it would be heard on the intercom. The argument ceased for a belated moment with the realisation of what Cockburn had uttered. The gate release clicked without explanation or further pause in the argument. Cockburn shrugged at Bolton. They pushed the gate open and walked to the front door. The muffled sound of the argument grew from behind the door as they approached.

Again, the door opened as Cockburn reached for the buzzer. Mansur Habdoud held the door open to expose Rashida Habdoud in full haranguing mode. The flood of daylight drew her to a sudden conclusion.

'Bah,' she said, flinging both palms downward in a dismissive gesture and turned back into the house.

Mansur Habdoud straightened his shoulders in an attempt to switch from harangue-ee to defiant crime family patriarch. The thin remnants of his black hair were slicked backwards from his lengthening forehead. He wore a mid-green polo top and loose, brown trousers. The striped navy blue slippers were the antithesis of gangster chic.

'I come. It is better that a doctor, priest or policeman does not enter your house.'

'Do you want to know what this is about?' Cockburn asked.

'You tell my lawyer. We'll be there in an hour.'

'You won't be able to see Eugene or Stephen before then.'

'You leave my boys outta this. Whatever it is, they had nothing to do with it. You think I wouldn't know if they killed some fucking dickhead?'

* * *

'My client has no knowledge of a murder and unless he is a suspect he does not wish to have this interview recorded.'

Adnan Androus's voice resonated with compelling richness somewhere between Henry Kissinger and Barry White. The towering figure with a full head of black hair and glowing bronzed face cut an all-pervading presence. He slung his slim leather satchel offhandedly onto the table and took a seat beside Mansur Habdoud. Mansur wore a tweedy brown jacket over his polo shirt. Scuffed brown shoes had replaced his house slippers.

'We have an interview room available with full recording facilities,' Cockburn said. 'If we tape it, there can be no argument about what was said.'

'No thank you inspector, and my client does not wish to have an interpreter present.'

Cockburn was following the routine suggested by Sergeant Bolton. They reasoned that if Adnan and Mansur felt they were successful in escaping police desire to record the interview or have an interpreter present, then Adnan and Mansur would feel comfortable enough to have mid-interview exchanges in Lebanese Arabic. An interpreter was nevertheless present behind the mirrored glass to take note of those conversations — if they occurred. This particular interpreter was nervous about participating in a Habdoud matter. Bill Bolton joined Cockburn to conduct the interview.

'Thank you for attending the interview Mr Habdoud. I'm investigating the death of Marcel Chabanne with whom you may have been acquainted. When I'm finished asking you about that, Sergeant Bolton will want to ask you about the pistol found in your car this morning.'

Adnan said something to Mansur in Lebanese.

Mr Habdoud does not know a Marcel Chabanne,' Adnan told Cockburn.

I need Mr Habdoud to answer the questions himself, Mr Androus. If he insists on speaking Lebanese then I am happy to wait until we find an interpreter.'

'Then ask him Inspector Cockburn,' Adnan said.

Cockburn ignored being mis-called inspector again and left his gaze on Adnan, trying to detect whether "Cockburn" had been emphasised. He decided not and asked Mansur, 'Do you know Marcel Chabanne who lives in a stone house along the Echuca Road from Heathcote?'

'Little Marcel? The eggman?'

'So you do know him?'

'Yes,' Mansur said with dismay. 'Marcel is dead?'

Adnan asked Mansur something in Lebanese. Mansur appeared to eagerly explain who Marcel was.

'My client says he does know who Marcel Chabanne is. He is someone he became casually acquainted with on his travels to the family's weekend property on the Murray River near Echuca. He is not someone that Mr Habdoud or his family have dealings with.'

'How did he die?' Mansur asked Cockburn.

Cockburn ignored the three-way conversation, content to know that the exchanges between Adnan and Mansur now flowed freely.

'He appears to have broken his neck in a fall. At this stage the death is being treated as suspicious.'

'Was he looking for eggs?' Mansur asked.

'What do you know about Marcel Chabanne's interest in egg collecting?'

Adnan spoke animatedly to Habdoud in Lebanese. Mansur fired a lengthy response back. Finally, Adnan explained.

'My client says he has an innocent acquaintance with the dead man. He is indeed upset to learn of his death. He is only too agreeable to explain his acquaintance if it will assist you in finding who might be responsible.'

Cockburn again held Adnan's gaze to impart his thought: *You're full of shit.*

'How were you acquainted with Marcel Chabanne, Mr Habdoud?'

'We went to his house because my daughter Nina wanted to buy it. She wanted to have it for gift shop. She and her friend who runs a shop in Northland talked her mother into it. They want to own Marcel's house for gift and coffee shop in the middle of fucking nowhere. And it peasant house overgrown with all sorts of shit. Donkey is donkey even if it carries the Sultan's treasure. I told her I could buy some land and build proper shop. Bricks and aluminium windows and paved car parking. Build it somewhere where people go — not in no man's land. But Rashida and Nina have to have the peasant house.'

'Your daughter wanted you to buy Marcel's house?'

'Yes. She wanted me to make offer.'

'Don't take that the wrong way sergeant,' Adnan chipped in.

'When did you make an offer to buy the house?'

'Not for long time and not to Marcel. He not own the house. No one can give what he does not have.'

'But you did meet Marcel?'

'The first coupla times, me and Rashida and Nina go there. No one answers door. Little Marcel lives on his own and he is shy boy. Very shy boy. But he comes on his bike when we stop there one day. He makes us tea and shows us his eggs. He is not so shy talking about eggs. He tells us how he finds eggs. He shows us nest in tree at back of his house. He climbs up there. Like that.' Mansur snapped his fingers. 'He is like monkey.'

'And he told you he wasn't the actual owner of the house.'

'He says the house in his family for more than hundred years. It must stay that way forever he says.'

'And that was too long for you to wait?'

'Sergeant Cockburn …' Adnan protested.

Mansur halted Adnan in Lebanese with some kind of explanation after which Adnan gestured with his hand for Mansur to continue.

'It was good that little Marcel didn't want to sell the house. It means I can escape Nina's stupid gift shop. But Nina and Rashida want me to try harder. Find his mother and father because they own the house. Rashida says only one thing for sure is change. She thinks I can make them sell.'

'She wants you to heavy them?'

'That's enough,' Adnan protested, only to be cut off by Mansur's answer.

'No. Not like that. Rashida wants me to ask the person who *owns* the house — not the tenant. The organ grinder, not the monkey. So Eugene finds where they live in Melbourne and we go and ask them. They still say no. Is win win for me,' Mansur smiled.

'What exactly did you ask them?'

'For Nina we will pay them good price. Eugene asks them why they won't sell the house for good price. They say it is their history. Their grandfather's grandfather built the house with his own hands. It is impossible for them not to keep it. It is Marcel's home now and they cannot take it away from Marcel.

'Eugene says we can make Marcel new house with everything in it. But they say that would be bad. Eugene tells them bad can be good if worse happens. We can make sure nothing bad happens, he tells them. That is all. They thinking about this and I tell Eugene we will go before they change their mind and sell it to us.' Mansur laughed.

During Mansur's admission, Adnan sat with elbows on the table and gripped his head with his fingertips. He sat up with a loud sigh to say, 'I hope you're not fishing for a motive for murder Sergeant. What my client described is merely a clash of culture. I trust you or the Chabannes have not misinterpreted the situation.'

'I imagine the death of their son at the property may have created more than enough desire for the Chabannes to divest themselves of the house.'

'If that's what you think, then you need to start looking for someone who actually wants the property. My client has been frank enough to describe his strong desire *not* to acquire the house. I hope you don't take that lightly.'

'Where were you on Tuesday three weeks ago, Mr Habdoud?'

Adnan and Mansur talked in Lebanese before Adnan answered, 'Mr Habdoud has not been away from Melbourne midweek for months. He will need to check his diary and calendar to get you the exact details of his movements on that day.'

'If you could, please, Mr Habdoud … and is there anything or anyone you know of or anything you noticed about Marcel or his house that might indicate why he was killed?'

'No. I am saddened by it. Me and Rashida and Nina … we called again to see Marcel and he made us tea again. We liked him. The greatest loss is what dies in us.'

Cockburn and Bolton entered the room adjoining the interview room. The now empty table and chairs were visible through the one-way glass.

'Who invited you?' Cockburn said when he saw Rory sitting with the smartly dressed female interpreter.

'Bourke,' Rory answered.

Cockburn switched his attention to the interpreter.

'What did they say?'

'Nothing that you wouldn't have gathered from what they said in English. Mansur seemed genuinely surprised by the news. He said "sadiq" often. It means friend. It sounded like he actually liked Marcel.'

'What about the long explanation he gave to Adnan?'

'He told Adnan not to worry. He said this is nothing to do with Eugene and Stephen or any of the family business. Eugene and Stephen have never met Marcel or been to his house. This is nothing to do with anything. That's why they are not arresting me, he said.'

'And what about the house?'

'He told Adnan what he told you. He thinks the house is a peasant shit hole. It is made of stones from the field and wood that is not even sawn properly. Stones are on the roof. He would be embarrassed to own it. It would cost him more than a new house to put a proper iron roof on it and fit aluminium windows. He lived in a rural hovel when he was a boy and he would not go back.'

'He says Eugene did not meet Marcel but he *did* meet his mum and dad,' Rory said. 'And have you seen Eugene? I reckon most people would feel threatened if he asked them the time of day. Maybe the Chabannes got the wrong end of the stick with this one.'

'You know what I heard and what I think?' Cockburn said with glances at Rory and the interpreter. 'Mansur knew all about Marcel's penchant for climbing trees for birds' eggs. Don't forget who we're dealing with. This moɔ shoot and bomb anyone who stands in their way. When you've got someone like that telling you "bad can be good if worse happens", you're not left in any doubt. That's not a culture difference — the meaning is plain in any language.'

'And you think Mansur would happily volunteer that conversation if it was meant to be a threat?' Rory argued.

'This is the Habdouds. They wouldn't need to drop Marcel from a height to break his neck and it's not beyond their simple minds to place him under a bird nest. I wanna find out exactly where Eugene and Stephen were on Tuesday three weeks ago.'

Rory took the lift back to his office. He retrieved the folded link diagram from his satchel and pinned it to the pinboard. Under the question mark that denoted the prospective coaching house purchaser he wrote "Habdouds".

As Rory pondered the diagram, tapping his chin with the permanent marker, Hamish Lynott came to his door. Hamish was the civilian manager of the Commercial and Electronic Branch IT boffins who surrounded Rory's office. As the sharpest knife in the drawer, Hamish broke the IT-mole mould in every way necessary to become their manager in his early 30s. For a start he wore a fitted suit without pleats in the trousers *and* a fitted shirt. However, it was his energy and compelling looks that most impressed.

'We've got a real white board if you want to borrow it,' Hamish offered.

'Thanks, but I need this to be portable.'

Rory was developing tea-room acquaintanceships with his fellow office floor occupants and Hamish had begun to go out of his way to have peer chats with Rory. *Perhaps Bourke had a hand in that*, Rory thought cynically — or self doubtingly.

'Tough case?' Hamish asked with his head cocked quizzically at Rory's diagram.

'That's the nature of all cold cases. Something from someone else's too hard basket.'

'I suppose so,' he said, before giving up on the diagram. He turned to Rory and told him, 'Haley is leaving tomorrow. She's joining one of the banks.'

'Which one's Haley? I'm still putting names to faces around here.'

'She's the lanky one, always in jeans. Anyway, we're having a counter lunch at the Locarno Hotel. We wondered if you wanted to join us.'

'Sorry, Hamish. I'm going to Bendigo tomorrow. But I appreciate the invite.'

'Anything we can help you with?' Hamish said, casting an eye to the tatty link diagram. 'I could get someone to transcribe it onto your laptop.'

'I'm too old-school for that. I wouldn't know how to update it.'

'We could show you how to do that too. It's a piece of piss.'

Rory studied the diagram and realised just how archaic it must appear to a gen X or Y or whatever Hamish belonged to.

'There's one thing on there that I drew a blank on. Do you mind if I ask you?'

'Shoot.'

Rory stood up and tapped the "Lady's Pass Run art museum development" box with the marker.

'This is a mega proposal called the Lady's Pass Museum of Art gallery resort. It's going to be built in the Heathcote wine region. No sod has been turned yet. They're dealing with the Government to get whatever breaks they can — tax breaks, fast-track planning, access roads, tourism promotion, that sort of stuff. The hotel was going to go under the Novamont banner but Novamont pulled the pin. The consortium have since secured another hotel chain but I'm curious to know why Novamont dropped out. The Department of Regional Development hit a brick wall. Is this something you could sus out?'

'Give me their website and a couple of days.'

Chapter 18

'Living the retirement dream?'

'Rory? What are you doing here?

'Moira told me where to find you.'

'If you came looking for me tomorrow you would have had to drive to Broken Hill.'

'I know, Moira was packing the caravan.'

Rory had spotted Eric Clement, formerly Sergeant Clement, before he braked and parked. The practice fairway of the Bendigo Golf Club ran alongside Golf Course Road and Eric and his dog Buster had it to themselves — and a good few other holes if they wanted them. The only other visible human was a distant groundsman driving a tractor-drawn mower. Nine years of de-stressing had shaken off the perpetual worried look that Eric bore throughout his work life. Or maybe the extra weight had ironed a few creases out, Rory supposed.

'Good to see you. I heard you were having a rough trot after the shooting. You okay now?'

'Been back at work for a couple of weeks now. But look at you. I reckon you look younger. How do you do that?'

Buster cautiously approached and sniffed Rory, decided he was friendly, and began licking his fingers.

'Not retiring isn't everything it's cracked up to be, I reckon.'

Rory had to think about it before saying, 'You can say that again.'

Eric reached with his eight iron to separate a ball from the pile at his feet. He chipped it towards the flag where it joined another six already spread across the green.

'Wow. You haven't missed any. What are you playing off these days?'

'Nine. I finally cracked single figures.'

'There's hope for us all.'

'I presume this is not a social call … being the first time you've come to see me since I retired.'

'It can be a social call. What time do they open the bar in there?'

Rory gave a nod towards the clubhouse. Eric looked at his watch and said, 'All right. I've got the day off.'

Eric led Rory to a window seat where they watched two forty-something women golfers tee off from the first. The room was empty other than the barman re-stacking a fridge.

'They've put me in charge of cold cases.'

'And you're looking at the Archie Ballantyne case,' Eric guessed.

'You haven't lost it,' Rory smiled. 'You did ask me to follow it up for you, if you remember.'

'That was nine years ago.'

'I had to make sure it was cold first,' Rory quipped and sipped from his pot of beer. 'The file jumped at me from the pile. The name must have stuck after you got in my ear about it at your retirement do.'

'It's taken all this time for me to discover that I didn't waste my breath. Have you found out anything yet?'

'I wasn't hopeful, but Seabridge stumbled across another supposed accident victim the very day I turned up to begin re-investigating. You probably heard about it. It was a bloke that fell from a tree.'

'I *didn't* hear about that. But Seabridge … isn't he the bloke who found Archie's body?'

'The very person. How intriguing is that?'

'Very intriguing. Do you know if it's connected?'

'Only if you go back a century or two. I found out that the dead bloke's ancestor once had a connection with Archie Ballantyne's land, which is now owned by Seabridge.'

'History and land. I remember saying that to you too. Do you remember?'

'I do remember. But I'm not sure any of that will have anything to do with the latest murder. It's a Bendigo CIU case and they've unearthed a connection with some hard-core Melbourne crims.'

Eric paused from sipping his beer to say, 'So why come and see me about it? You're not here to give me false hope that Archie Ballantyne's murder will be solved, are you?'

'No. I wanted to get your ideas about how someone could have killed Archie. As you know, there was not much hypothesising done by the Homicide detectives who took over the case. Or none they recorded on file.'

'They knew my thoughts well enough.'

'Can you remember enough to tell me how you think something like that could be done?'

'Shit yeah. The whole thing could be easily set up if Archie was whacked on the head first. Then, whoever did it could switch off the electricity connection to the shed. This can be done from the meter box at the house. They would have put Archie's body in the shed bay where the forty-four-gallon drum of petrol was stored. Archie's angle grinder could then be plugged in and the trigger lock switch engaged. The angle grinder blade resting on the piece of steel would give off a shower of sparks the moment the power was turned back on at the meter box.

'The drum of petrol had a hand pump fitted, which meant it was virtually unsealed. The murderer would have pumped a bit into the hose and placed the nozzle beside the angle grinder. They of course would be safely out of range at the house when they threw the switch. It wouldn't have mattered if Archie was unconscious or already dead because any prior injuries were taken to have occurred in the explosion and fire.'

'How did this check out on site?'

'One of the first things the fire brigade did was switch off the electricity at the meter box, so there were no fingerprints or any other way of telling if this actually happened. The explosion and fire was so great that it was impossible to glean if the body was harmed beforehand. There were no other vehicle tracks into the place other than Seabridge's and because he appeared entirely motive free, he was not seriously considered a suspect. The sale of the property between Archie and Seabridge had been amicably settled that very day. Both conveyancing solicitors confirmed that. Seabridge had no other history or connection to Archie.'

Rory picked up Eric's line of thought. 'As things turned out, Seabridge harboured no interest in any of Archie's other land. It was sold off to others when Archie's estate was eventually settled. Seabridge did, however, buy the house block when it came back on the market some years later. But it's hardly a scenario he could have expected to unfold as a result of murdering Archie. And yet, here he is again, stumbling across a murder that someone tries to pass off as an accident.'

'Perhaps he's simply accident prone,' Eric kidded.

'Let's hope so. I'd like to see him come a cropper.'

Each mulled the riddle as they watched the female golfers silently search the rough for their tee shots.

'A moment ago you told me I haven't lost it,' Eric said at last.

'Yeah?' Rory said diffidently.

'You're right. There *are* things you don't lose when you retire. The first person a copper books for speeding starts spinning them a story. You spend the rest of your time trying to read people.'

'You're not talking about Seabridge, are you?'

'No. The thing with you shooting someone — you might as well have it tattooed on your forehead.'

Rory rubbed his neck. When Rory was a constable in need of a reprimand, Eric always found a way to be encouraging. Now he felt a sting in Eric's words — and he wasn't his supervising officer or even a policeman any more.

'It's not something I can switch off and on, Eric,' Rory muttered.

'I don't know what the shrinks told you, but you weren't wired to kill anyone. Not many cops are, despite the training. You had a lot of things going for you but dealing with killing someone was not one of them. None of us can have it all.'

'Even a bit would be handy right now.'

'There was a time when I thought you *did* have it all. When I bailed you up about the Archie Ballantyne case at my farewell. You probably thought I was pissed but I remember every word I told you. I said the case needs someone smart like you. I also said you stood out from the pack on your first day on the job. You were sharp, insightful … even the good looks didn't go astray. *And* you had a bit of cunning, I liked that too. Not rat-cunning like Cockburn. He wouldn't have any trouble shooting someone — he's probably jealous it wasn't him. No, your shrewdness came from intelligence, patient observation, persistence. You were a born investigator.'

'Were.'

'We're all human in the end. We all live with the chance that a weakness will be exposed. But remember, you didn't lack bravery and you didn't become un-smart all of a sudden. I know something dies inside but you don't have to be someone your colleagues talk about behind your back. You've still got everything you need to make a mark in the job, and you've re-found some will. Maybe you've even gained some perverse insight from all this. If you crack this case or get a promotion, then they'll only ever talk about you for the right reasons. Don't waste the chance you've been given.'

'Promotion is the last thing on my mind.'

'That's your problem. When you tee off over water, are you thinking about avoiding the water or are you thinking about landing on the green? Remember what the great golfer Sam Snead said, "Of all hazards, fear is the worst".'

'Have you cracked your case or is this a special occasion I don't know about?' Sigrid asked.

They were seated in the Whirrakee Restaurant — Bendigo's first restaurant in over a decade to be awarded a chef's hat by *The Age Good Food Guide*. The prized window seat of the historic bank building framed the heart of Bendigo with everything that made it "Vienna in the

Bush". The opulent classical domes and towers of Pall Mall were a legacy of the town's immense gold-mining wealth. At its forefront was the marble marvel of Princess Alexandra Fountain — sitting centre stage for Whirrakee diners.

A half flight of steps took diners above the height of passing pedestrians. The city's lights added mesmeric elegance to the grandeur. A glowing restaurant tram trundled through the massive intersection as Rory answered, 'If I had cracked the case, I wouldn't be here now.'

'So why not the Boundary Hotel — our "usual"?' Sigrid said, smoothing the linen table-cloth edge. She wore an unbuttoned mini cardigan over a glossy printed dress — the matching belt did its job of showing her figure. A silver pendant hung above a restrained vee neckline that delved to the uppermost parting of her breasts. Rory sported a new pair of black casual trousers.

'I had a golf lesson today. Apparently I'm not aiming high enough.'

'And you're hoping this will somehow improve your handicap?' Sigrid cast her eyes around the room showily.

'Something like that.'

'I can talk in riddles all night if you like.'

'Do you mind if I get the other night out of the way now?'

'You don't have to explain yourself.'

'I want to. Especially if we're going to see more of each other.'

The waitress returned with their drinks and asked if they were ready to order.

'Sorry, we haven't got to the menu yet,' Rory answered.

'I'll be back in a while,' she said and headed to the small bar.

'You were going to tell me …' Sigrid prompted.

'This thing with me shooting someone last year. You've probably gathered that I was badly affected. In fact, I only returned to work when I came up here on this case. I thought I had mended but I copped a rude reminder on that first day. It brought back the nightmares I'd managed to shake off. None of the other symptoms returned. Just the nightly nightmare.'

'Is it still happening.'

'Not every night. But it's something I'll have to learn to live with. The thing was, the thought of sleeping with you scared me because the nightmare would happen if I stayed and fell asleep afterwards. It's not a pretty thing. I wake up blathering all sorts of hysterical crap … even crying. I'm so lathered in sweat I have to have a shower there and then. It would freak you right out. It freaks me out.'

'I understand,' she said and reached for his hand. 'I appreciate that you were concerned for me.'

'So if …' He paused unable to find the words to delicately say or infer having sex.

'So if I kiss you again, I know you will be concerned for me?' she goaded.

'After my golf lesson, I might aim even higher.'

She realised she still had her hand on his. She pressed it, looked at him sincerely and said, 'Let's see what's on the menu, shall we?'

'How about French champagne?'

'It sounds good to me. I thought you may have preferred a local red.'

'Too much like work at the moment.'

Sigrid ordered the roasted duck breast; Rory the wild barramundi.

'And I've got you here all week?'

'I would have been heading back sooner but I've got a funeral in Bendigo at the end of the week.'

Her glossy nakedness swamped Rory's lust-starved skin. A year in the sexual wilderness did nothing to curb or inhibit his performance. Moreover, long-suppressed appetite filled with hitherto unknown ferocity. Sigrid's breathy synchronised moans became equally urgent. Before they both knew it, their latent ecstasies were un-protractible.

'It's been too long for both of us,' Sigrid announced as they fell apart to contemplate the darkness of the four-poster bed canopy. Her body shone in the street light that crept through the window. He reached across to place his hand on her hip. He needed to continue the realness of it.

'Can you imagine never experiencing something like this again?' he asked into the darkness.

'I try not to.'

'The thought has been going around in my head since I passed up the chance the other night.'

'They say the one you pass up is the one you never catch up on.'

'Well I passed up on one. What if it kept happening?'

Sigrid raised herself on an elbow to look at him. 'I can tell you now, there was no way you were ever going to hold that hurricane inside. That was something.'

'Yeah?' he asked smugly.

She rose from the bed.

'Where are you going?'

'I won't do the nightmare thing. Not now you've told me.'

'Is that why you insisted coming to my room? You were never going to stay all night, were you?'

'I could if you wanted me to, but I don't hear you trying to change my mind. I honestly don't mind.'

The streetlight cast teasing black silk shadows onto her body. The darkness spread from her breasts as she leant over to kiss him goodnight. Cause and effect were instant. He pulled her back on to him.

Chapter 19

Three chimneys were all that remained of the house where Archie was born. The chimneys' elaborate corbel brick crowns suggested an original homestead of some lavishness. Its 1950s successor, where Archie lived all his adult life, stood fifty metres to its left. The triple-fronted cream brick-veneer mould was also lavishly exceeded with an additional frontage, rounded corner windows and an art deco-shaped upper storey and balcony. Wide circular concrete steps cascaded from the front entrance. The generous interpretation of an Australian classic was from a time before wool ceased being Australia's major source of export income.

The shed where Archie died was a hundred metres beyond the house, with Mount Camel as its backdrop. The Colorbond replacement had been re-erected on the original concrete slab.

The cream brick home was fenced like a suburban house. Rory parked by the gate in the front fence. The name "Kirkhill" was embossed on a decorative copper panel fitted to a headboard above the gate — retrieved from the original homestead, no doubt. He noticed Seabridge's Toyota Hilux by a gate in the side fence that led to the back door. Rory circled the front yard where a few hardy roses and gazanias clung desperately to life after a decade of drought and neglect. The side gate hung open below a vigorous wisteria to expose an enclosed back yard of leafy fruit trees scattered around a dry lawn. He followed the concrete path through a painted pergola to the open back entrance and gave a rattling knock on the side of the screen door.

'Detective James. I didn't hear you arrive,' Seabridge said.

'Sorry. I parked at the front gate and ended up walking to the back door.'

'Well, come in.'

He led Rory through a boots-and-coats lobby to the large kitchen. The 1950s painted Masonite cupboards with black plastic and chrome fittings had barely seen change. The non-window side of the room was dominated by an oversized slow combustion cooker set below a broad canopy. The row of cupboards to its right had been shortened to include a modern electric stove and oven. Mount Camel was dominant through the expansive window above the sink on the opposite wall.

Seabridge noticed Rory's admiring scan of the room.

'This place defied the trend when kitchens began to shrink. It's a gem.'

'I'll say.'

'Archie was never going to renovate the place after his wife died and nor did the subsequent owner — thankfully. We'd love to keep it the way it is. We did install the modern cooker and we're considering central heating. It's heated by open fires, hence my trip into the forest when I found Marcel.'

Rory glanced around the room, hands in the pockets of his new suit and with the demeanor he wished he had on his first meeting with Seabridge. He noticed his resolve returning each morning as the razor peeled shaving cream from his face. The lines deepened somewhat, lips now a bit grimmer, but his hair was still dark and ruffled the way he liked it — if only he could have started all this bearing the same determined and knowing look.

'Have you lived here long?'

'No. We bought the place to expand our vineyard and we rented this out for a few years. When the resort development idea came about, we converted our accommodation at the cellar-door building into a project office. Now Ursula and I stay here when we come up.'

'Thanks for sparing the time to show me where you found Archie.'

'That's all right, Detective. It's beyond my imagination how you hope to shed new light on something that happened fourteen years ago. I mean, I understand how DNA can reveal the past with utter precision but surely any other physical clues must fade quickly, or even slowly, with time.'

'I don't expect to bend over and pick up something that escaped the notice of my predecessors. This is seeing for myself how something like that happened.'

'Mm,' Seabridge said. 'Shall I take you over there?'

'I'd like to have a look at the electricity meter box before we go to the shed.'

'The meter box? I'm sure you know it wasn't an electrical fire Sergeant. I don't think anyone doubted that the fire was caused by the sparks from Archie's angle grinder.'

'Did you attend the inquest?'

'Of course. I gave my evidence about discovering the body.'

Rory crossed his arms and looked down to gather his words.

'There's a theory that wasn't put forward at the inquest about how the accident could be set up by some other person.'

'Oh?'

Rory explained Eric's theory. About how the angle grinder, the petrol, the body could all be set in place — ready to be triggered at the house meter box. Rory studied Seabridge's face as he espoused Eric's theory. It was only noteworthy by the lack of any reaction.

'I'm not surprised that it wasn't mentioned at the inquest. It sounds like … well, I don't know what it sounds like. Wouldn't you need to find someone who wanted to kill Archie if you were going to create elaborate methodologies to fit the circumstances?'

'Of course we need someone with a motive. And it is mystifying why someone would want to kill Archie.'

'Perhaps that's a clue that it was an accident after all.'

'The possibility certainly wasn't ruled out by the Coroner, but nor was it ruled in. Why don't you show me the meter box in any case.'

Seabridge led Rory through the house and out the front double doors that opened from an expansive entry hall. The original floral carpet had worn well.

'Here it is,' Seabrook said pointing to the timber meter box that sat alongside the front door like a feature. Inside the box, several round Bakelite switches were positioned below two rows of ceramic fuse holders. The word "SHED" was written in white ink below one of the switches mounted on the black backing board.

'That looks straightforward. A would-be killer wouldn't have trouble working that out. I don't suppose you noticed anything about the switchboard on the day?'

'No. I didn't even stop at the house when I arrived because the smoke from the shed caught my eye. I did come to the back door to phone the police and fire brigade on the land line. There was no reception here on my mobile phone in those days. But I didn't go anywhere near the meter box — so I didn't notice anything about it. I know the fire brigade turned off the electricity when they arrived. I presume they did that at the meter box.'

'I see. You'd better take me to the scene then.'

As they walked the track from the house to the shed, Rory asked, 'Was there much smoke when you arrived that day?'

'Not a lot. It had reached the smouldering stage. I couldn't find a fire extinguisher or hose, so I did what I could bucketing water from the shed tank. Mainly on Archie's body.'

'Did you do that before or after you phoned?'

Seabridge stopped to look at Rory.

'I phoned first, Detective. Archie's body was charred to a crisp by then. There was no question of checking his pulse or giving CPR. It was hard enough seeing him like that.'

They began walking again.

'Did it cross your mind that he might have been murdered?'

'Absolutely not.'

'From the photographs I've seen, it wouldn't have been apparent to the untrained eye that the fire was caused by an angle grinder. What were your first thoughts about how the explosion happened? Something usually jumps into people's minds, however unlikely.'

Seabridge stopped again.

'It's not uncomfortable for you to talk about, is it?' Rory added.

'No. I don't mind. I see the shed every day when we stay here.'

'And you don't recall what you first imagined when you discovered the fire and Archie's body?'

'Murder certainly never crossed my mind. I know the firemen took it to be a farm workshop accident. I suppose I did too.'

They came to a halt in front of the four-bay shed. Sliding doors were drawn back to reveal hay stacked to the ceiling in one and a half bays. A ride-on mower and hand tools were stored in the third bay from which a doorway led to a workshop.

'This is the original concrete slab, I take it?' Rory asked.

'Yes. The subsequent owners had the shed rebuilt as soon as they bought the place. You can still see fire marks on the floor when it's empty. The explosion happened below that pile of hay. We buy that in for the alpacas.'

'And where was the body?'

'The original shed had a steel dividing wall between those two bays. The force of the explosion must have thrown Archie against that wall. He was about half way towards the back of the shed.'

'And the angle grinder?'

'It was near where the drum exploded. It was a melted blob.'

'I understand a pile of fencing material had been delivered the previous day. Do you remember where that was placed?'

'The fencing material?' Seabridge's face twisted somewhere between surprise and annoyance. 'What's that got to do with anything?'

'That's what I'd like to find out. No one knew why Archie bought 450 metres of fencing and a gate. Especially when he was selling off land. All his existing fences were in good order. Maybe it's a clue about why someone would murder him.'

'I presume he was going to subdivide some of his larger paddocks.'

'Did he tell you that?'

'No,' Seabridge said in an irritated tone. 'I didn't get to know Archie well. I first met him about a year before he sold the land to me. I visited him a few times after that as I tried to persuade him to sell the old vineyard block. That's what we talked about mainly. He told me about the history of the place and about his wife dying twelve years earlier. He spoke about his life slowing down but I'm afraid we didn't talk about his farming operations at all.'

'So do you remember where the fencing material was on the day you found him?' Rory asked

'It was stacked over there.'

He pointed resignedly.

'Did you notice other vehicle tracks or footprints before the fire brigade attended?'

'For fuck's sake. What is this?' Seabridge burst out. He drove his hands into his pockets and stepped closer to Rory. The usual accompanying gestures were abruptly replaced by a pushed-up chin and chillingly raised eyelids.

'Your colleagues went through all of this fourteen years ago. Do you think I did it and you're waiting for me to slip up and say something different? I've taken time out to show you the scene and I've done that in good faith. If you're treating me as some kind of suspect … aren't you supposed to tell me or let me have a lawyer or something? Shouldn't you at least have an offsider to back your story?'

Rory feigned surprise and paused to absorb the length of Seabridge's tether.

'I'm sorry Mr Seabridge. I'm getting carried away with the scene of the crime, if that's what it is. I certainly wasn't fishing for suspects. Not yet. And if it does turn out to be a murder, there's still no one we know of yet with a motive.'

'What about some of the locals? There are farmers around here who hold strong views about how the traditional farming landscape is being destroyed by vineyards. Those that are not on the Cambrian soil become jealous when they discover the price that the farmers on the red soil get from wine growers. All of them envy the success that wine growers have in making money from the land. And what about Archie's in-laws who inherited the place? They didn't waste any time turning it into hard cash. There was no emotional attachment there.'

'So you *do* think someone murdered Archie?'

Seabridge was struck silent with the realisation of what his ire had led him to say.

'No,' he said, when he had gathered his thoughts. 'I'm answering your question about who may have had reason to kill him. That doesn't mean I thought they did it.'

'I see. It's been helpful to see where it happened. I appreciate that you made yourself available. Particularly for something so horrific.'

'It's something I never want to come across again.'

'You needed to be careful what you wished for Mr Seabridge.'

Rory answered the call on his hands-free.

'Hamish Lynott here, where are you?'

'Driving through Knowsley, and don't tell me you've never heard of it.'

'I've never heard of it.'

'I suppose I asked for that.'

'I'd trade places today, wherever it is. You wouldn't believe the shit that is going down since the Ardoz Securities thing hit the headlines this morning. I did manage to find something about the Novamont thing though. I thought I'd better let you know before I get roped into the Ardoz Securities frenzy for the rest of the week.'

'Is the Novamont thing significant?'

'Don't get your hopes up. I couldn't find out why Novamont pulled the pin on their involvement in the Lady's Pass project. Dominique did however discover the names of two consultant firms that did some due diligence checks for them. One of them is a surveying company just down the road from here. Dominique just happens to know one of the surveyors who work there. He remembered an anomaly being discovered about the land. Apparently the actual boundary fence did not match the land title. There was a discrepancy of forty acres.'

'So what happened?'

'Probably nothing. Novamont were already talking about quitting by the time the surveyors submitted their report. The firm heard nothing more about it.'

'Do you have anything you can email me?'

'I've got a scan of the original Certificate of Title on screen now. It's Crown Allotment 56 in the Parish of Redcastle. The area shown on the title is eighty acres and a few roods and perches. However, when the surveyors measured the paddock, they came up with one hundred and twenty acres.'

'I assume you're talking English?'

'Roods and perches are proportions of an acre. You'll learn when you chase this stuff down. I presume you already know that "Crown" refers to the State and "Parish" is how each local district is defined.'

'What does it all mean?'

'It means that Seabridge might not have a land title for forty of the acres he occupies.'

'It sounds like a black hole. How do I check something like that out?'

'You need to find a copy of the parish plan to see where the discrepancy is. There'll be one at the local Land Victoria office. I think you'll find they're part of the Department of Sustainability and Environment. In the meantime, I'll email you a scan of the land title.'

'Thanks, Hamish. I owe you one.'

'One other thing, Rory. Someone delivered a box for you this morning. Were you expecting anything? It's sitting on your desk.'

'Oh?'

'I can open it if you like.'

'Thanks,' Rory said, still mystified.

'I'm in your office now. I'll just put the phone on speaker.'

Rory listened to the sound of tearing wrapping paper subside to paper shuffling noises.

'Mm …'

'What?'

'Hang on Rory, I'm trying to figure it out. Talk amongst yourself.'

After a half a kilometre passed, Hamish began to laugh loudly.

'You won't believe what I think it is.'

'It can't be that funny. What?'

'It looks to me like someone has sent you a box of French letters.'

Chapter 20

Fern Baillie spread the giant Land Victoria parish plan across the meeting room table.

'It's all electronic these days,' she told Rory.

'I suppose there's an App for it,' Rory quipped.

'You look too young to be an old-school-everything baby boomer cynic.'

Fern was still on the right side of forty with the instant air of being well-organized. She wore her own personal two-piece grey office uniform. A timeless bob framed her barely made-up face.

'I thought I was keeping up until smart phones took over the world last week.'

'If you had to deal with old plans like this every day you'd soon be jumping on board. This is the Parish of Redcastle in the County of Rodney. What piece of land did you want to know about?'

Rory unfolded the email printout and read out, 'Crown Allotment 56'.

'There's Allotment 56, over near Mount Camel.'

'The Certificate of Title shows an area of eighty acres. Does that match the plan?'

'Nowhere near it. See that?'

The plan was like an oversized children's colour-by-numbers page. More than half the shapes were rectangles. The remainder were misshaped along one or more of their boundaries by winding roads, streams or other unmarked natural features. Each shape was labelled in its centre with a name and set of three numbers. Rory followed Fern's finger to Allotment 56. It read "J. A. Ballantyne", below which were the figures "119 . 3 . 26".

'That's 119 acres, three roods and twenty-six perches. Fourteen perches shy of 120 acres.'

'How can the same allotment be different?'

'Perhaps Allotment 56 was amalgamated with another piece of land, although it's unusual if not impossible for the Certificate of Title not to have also been changed if that were the case.'

Fern searched the plan intently for an explanation.

'Is it still in the name of Ballantyne?' she asked.

'It was until fourteen years ago. It's now owned by Seabridge. I'm told that a formal title search was recently done and everything checked out.'

'That wouldn't have identified any discrepancy in area. You would need to carry out an on-site survey to discover that.'

'That's exactly what happened a few months ago. But the company that organised the survey didn't proceed with their interest in the land. They didn't investigate the matter any further.'

'Do you have a copy of the title?'

'I've got a scanned copy here that I'm not supposed to have.'

Rory retrieved the printout from his satchel. The old document bore the royal coat of arms of the United Kingdom with a lion and a unicorn — a relic of colonial times that for some forgotten reason, is featured in the masthead of Melbourne's *The Age* newspaper to this day. The gothic font heading of "Certificate of Title" was underlined with the smaller words, "under the Transfer of Land Statute". The remainder of the document was handcrafted with nib and ink in a slanted cursive script:

John Archibald Ballantyne of Murray Road Mount Camel, Farmer, is now the proprietor of an Estate in Fee simple, subject to the Encumbrances notified hereunder in All that piece of Land, delineated and coloured red on the Map in the margin.

The red shape of the land was drawn on the lower left-hand side of the document.

Fern read the document to herself and placed it beside the parish plan. Rory watched her eyes dart from one to the other as she compared the rectangular shapes of the two Allotment 56s.

'It's the south end that's missing from the title. See … the shape of the land shown on the title matches the northern two thirds of Allotment 56 on the parish plan.

The southern end is missing from the original title. These figures along each side of the allotment on the parish plan are measurements in links. According to my rough calculations, the missing bit is about forty acres.'

'I think that's the original vineyard end.'

'I can't help you with that,' Fern said.

'Can you find out what has happened to the missing bit?'

'There should be a paper trail somewhere but it could take some time. And this could have happened any time during the past 150 years. Tracking it down will depend on how well it was documented. Earlier versions of the plan will provide the best clue about when it changed. This version was drawn in the 1970s.'

'Can we have a look at the earlier plans?'

'Not now, I'm afraid. They would have been archived in Melbourne decades ago. I can do a search and see what's available if you like. In the meantime, we have the Parish of Redcastle correspondence file. You're welcome to trawl through that if you've got plenty of time to spare. There are a few folders worth of stuff and there's no guarantee that it will include something like this. What's more, the file might not go all the way back to the 1860s when most of this land was first sold.

'I've got all day.'

'You'd better get yourself a cup of coffee then. I'll go and get you the files.'

* * *

Rory hit the wall by lunch time. The very nature of their task makes guardians of land records the Olympic champions of bureaucratese. They sat head and shoulders above other government departments for so regularly implanting "hereinafters" and "corresponding previous enactments" into general correspondence. Legal correspondents played the game well too. Even the untrained public found themselves compelled to insert what little jargon they garnered into their own handwritten letters. Such verbosity increased as Rory worked forward from the earliest record. The smudgy, almost transparent carbon copies and spidery scrawled letters and file notes gradually turned his brain to soup.

He marked his place in the file and despaired to see he was a mere centimetre into one of six bulging folders, each thicker than an Oxford dictionary. He then recollected that his other pile of information was written in French.

At least if I was knocking on doors I'd be meeting people, thought Rory. *The case has turned me into a backroom historian and now some kind of pre-computer age conveyancing clerk. It could be dangerous arming cops subjected to this for too long. And just how cold can a cold case get?*

'Fuck,' he announced to the empty meeting room. He sipped his second cup of coffee and idly opened the most recent file to see how the rise and fall of bureaucratese ended — if indeed it did end. The frequency of activity had at least slowed down. The most recent piece of correspondence was five years old. He half-heartedly flicked through the next dozen or so pages and abruptly paused mid page-turn when the words "Archie Ballantyne" leapt from the page.

It was a handwritten file note of less than a page in length.

Counter enquiry from Archie Ballantyne, owner of Crown Allotments 56 and 57 Parish of Redcastle.

Mr Ballantyne has identified that 40 acres of land contiguous with both these allotments is without title. It appears from the parish plan that the subject 40 acres had at some time been incorporated into Allotment 56 to reach a total of about 120 acres. However, only the northern eighty acres is shown on Mr Ballantyne's title for Allotment 56. The title clearly excludes the subject 40 acres, even though the boundary fence encompasses all of the 120 acres of land. According to Mr Ballantyne, his family have been in possession of the land in this manner for generations. Mr Ballantyne's possession for grazing purposes has occurred through the absence of a boundary fence between Allotment 56 (as defined by the title), and the subject land.

I advised Mr Ballantyne that if that is so, he may be in a position to acquire formal ownership, with title, by way of adverse possession. When I explained the adverse possession principle and process to Mr Ballantyne, he told me he is currently considering selling Allotment 56. I confirmed to him that a

The file note was signed by Claire Firebrace, Land Information Officer, and dated fifteen years earlier. After reading the file note twice, Rory went to reception to summon Fern Baillie.

'You're going to have to explain this to me.'

He watched a smile spread over her face as she read the file note.

'Ah. Adverse possession. That makes sense.'

'What's adverse possession?'

'It's an old doctrine that says, where a trespasser remains in possession of land for fifteen years to the exclusion of the true owner, then that person may have acquired ownership of the land. It often comes into play when a suburban fence line is found to be misaligned with the proper title boundary. In those cases, someone ends up gaining a sliver of their neighbour's land. But the law doesn't limit claims by the size of land — such as this case.'

Rory studied the ceiling as if trying to discern whether something was faintly written there.

'Does that explain it well enough?' she asked in a cautious tone.

He snapped back to the here and now. 'It explains a lot more as well. Can you tell me what the distance is along the boundary between the Allotment 56 title land and the adverse possession land?'

Fern leant over the parish plan and said almost instantly, '2224 four links … about 450 metres in the new.'

'Bingo,' Rory said with a fist-clenching forearm flex.

'Wow. Another extremely satisfied customer. Do you still want me to chase up the archived parish plans?'

'If you can, please. This is probably only half the story. And can I get a copy of the parish plan and this file note?'

'Sure, but if you're in a hurry, the Bendigo library has some of the historical sale plans on microfiche. That might be worth a try.'

Rory was becoming familiar with the layout of Crown allotments in the Parish of Redcastle. The library had several microfiche versions in negative film format of white text and lines on a blue background. One survey plan set out a group of allotments proclaimed open for selection. The library assistant explained to Rory that it was a copy of the original lithograph that prospective purchasers could obtain from the Land Office in Heathcote in the very early 1860s. Although the sale plan was yet to be populated with the purchasers' names, broad descriptions of the land were superimposed across various sections of the plan. Allotments closest to Mount Camel bore the description, "Rich reddish soil". The agricultural quality of the country diminished the further downslope and distant allotments were from Mount Camel. The most easterly read "Barren stony ranges. Box forest and scrub".

Rory quickly found Allotment 56 on the sale plan. It matched the size and shape drawn on the Certificate of Title. He eagerly cast his eye to the adjoining forty acres and found it was labelled Allotment 56A.

At last. This bit of land does have a legal identity — or an ex-identity at least.

Rory surmised that the vineyard began life as an allotment in its own right with its own number and at some point in the ensuing 150 years, the land office amalgamated Allotments 56 and 56A. *So why wasn't the title adjusted accordingly?*

He found himself staring hard at the sale plan as if the answer would jump from the microfiche screen. A thin rectangle of road alongside Allotment 57 caught his eye. He couldn't remember seeing it on the parish plan. He retrieved the parish plan that Fern Baillie had photocopied for him and found that it no longer existed. On close examination of the two plans, he could see that at some point in time, the access road to Allotment 56A had been incorporated into Allotment 57.

'Can you print me off a copy please?' he asked the library assistant.

'Hi Richard, it's Rory.'

'You blokes don't know how good you've got it,' Inspector Richard Bourke said into the speaker phone. Rory could hear him continue to tap the computer keyboard. 'I haven't been out of the office since you were last in here. What's the outside world like?'

'I've found something on the Archie Ballantyne case.'

'Have you?' he said into the sudden quiet. 'What?'

'It's complicated. Stuff to do with the land and Seabridge. I'll come back to Melbourne and brief you.'

'So Seabridge is our man?'

'I'm pretty sure.'

'Any connection with Marcel Chabanne?'

'Chabannes have a historical connection with the same piece of land. I'm talking more than 100 years ago. But it doesn't link Seabridge and Marcel Chabanne in the present day.'

'Have you spoken to Cockburn about any of this, or how he's doing with the Chabanne investigation?'

'No,' Rory said abruptly.

'Then get him here for this briefing too. Friday morning. I need everyone singing from the same hymn book, even if the cases turn out not to be connected.'

Rory's imagination could not stretch to Cockburn innocently singing hymns.

'Can we make it Monday morning? I have a funeral to go to in Bendigo.'

Chapter 21

Forty minutes early for a funeral. If he didn't catch Lauren when she arrived at the church they would not come face to face until Beryl's coffin was being carried out. Rory could imagine no poorer circumstance for a first meeting in over twelve months. There had been a couple of unavoidable phone calls but no first-hand encounters. They robbed each other of the facial expressions, gestures, eye movements and body posture that formed the bulk of communication. He knew Steph would have told her mother that she had asked him to come. Despite the gaping schism between them, Lauren knew she could rely on Rory to be there beforehand. Neither could shed the shared values of their eighteen year marriage.

The empty hearse was parked below the steps and some people Rory didn't recognise were already arriving. Reading the paper would be poor form. He envied the new generation that was permanently plugged into their iPod and iPhone to perpetually text and twitter. All he could do was stand around and not look conspicuous. *Why didn't the church install an outside pew for people like me?*

Rory was relieved to see Lauren's brother Peter accompanying their father, Keith. It meant that Lauren, Steph and Nick might arrive without other family members who he hoped to avoid. He acknowledged Peter and his father's surprised nods of greeting from a safe distance.

Lauren, Steph and Nick stepped from the next car that arrived. Lauren's scan of the church forecourt quickly fixed Rory's position as a direction to avoid looking in until the three stood at the base of the stairs cascading from the church doors. Rory realised there was no partner with Lauren and unnerved himself when he realised that it was a possibility he hadn't considered. *Could I have handled it? Hardly.*

Steph spotted Rory and ran in tears to throw her arms around him. Her more-womanly-by-the-minute face harshly reinforced how long it had been.

'I'm sorry, Dad. Thanks for coming,' she sobbed into his ear.

'It's all right. I'll always be here for you. You know that,' he said shakily, patting her back.

They broke apart but he kept his arm around Steph. It was contact he needed as much as she did. He was looking at Lauren, who was only centimetres away.

'I came for Steph, and Nick. I'll wait out here if you like.'

They say *living well is the best revenge*. If you're Lauren James, then *grow more attractive* is not a bad alternative strategy. With malice no longer spitting from her soft brown eyes, a sea of memories washed over Rory. She tilted her head knowingly at him.

'I'm so sorry about Beryl. She was so accepting of me from the day we met.'

'I know.' Lauren's first words to him.

She placed her arm around Nick who made no move towards Rory.

'Your grandmother was a remarkable person, Nick,' Rory said.

'I know,' Nick said without looking at his father.

'Come inside if you want, Rory. I don't mind if you sit down the back.'

Rory melted to the edge of the forecourt and watched familiar family faces emerge from the church. Lauren was absorbed into the huddle of pall bearers disassembling from their task. Her Rory moment had come and gone.

Nick was talking to cousins. Steph stood on the lower steps looking for Rory.

'Mum said I can go to the cemetery with you.'

It was no time to admit he hadn't intended to go to the graveside ceremony.

She held his arm as they watched the crowd disperse to their cars.

'It's a police car,' Steph observed once inside.

'Yeah.'

A comfortable silence settled until Steph asked, 'Mum and Nick said that killing that person made you unwell but now you're getting better.'

'It did send me on a bit of a downward spiral but I'm back at work now. I miss you and your brother.'

'And Mum?'

'Of course. But that was my own stupid fault. I can never claim that back. I can only learn to live with it.'

The silence came back.

'How's second year uni? What's the latest adventure in your Outdoor Education course?'

'I had to miss a Tasmanian wilderness field trip for the funeral.'

'Oh no, Steph.'

The cortege passed below the railway bridge where the train line and McIvor Road both crossed Back Creek. The nineteenth-century brick and bluestone abutments rose from the box-walled creek bed to road level and above that to the top of the railway embankment. Rory pointed to the small white patches scattered here and there on the rough-hewn bluestone pitchers.

'Do you know what those white patches are?'

'Yeah,' Steph said in a way that suggested it was a no-brainer.

'Well?'

'It's rock climbers chalk marks. They come here to boulder or practise traversing. We use chalk for grip. It absorbs sweat.'

'We?'

'Rock-climbing is one of our course skills, Dad. Why do the chalk marks interest you anyway? Is this a work question?'

'Kind of. I noticed some marks like those last week.'

'Where?'

'On the house wall of a bloke who did rock-climbing. It's a rough-stone house. They said he did free soloing.'

'Free soloing. Shit.'

'So what's free soloing? Is it anything like bouldering?'

'You don't use a rope for either but bouldering is not high off the ground … *and* you have a mat to land on if you fall. Free solo-ers are adrenalin-chasing junkies. They're the blokes who take on skyscrapers and the Northwest Face at Yosemite using nothing but their hands and feet. The difference between the two is living or dying.'

Rory left the engine running at the cemetery.

'Aren't you coming?'

'Your mother needs you now.'

'But I want to see you again.'

'I'll call you. We'll do something together.'

Steph kissed his cheek and reached across the console to give him a tight one-arm hug.

'Thanks for coming,' she sniffed.

Rory slid the passenger side window down as Steph stooped for their final words and asked, 'Hey, I noticed Jacky and Adele at the church. Are they still living on the corner of Searle Street?'

'I think so. I still see his car in the driveway whenever I'm home. Why do you ask?'

'I have some mail to drop in.'

Jacky Du Camp lived a couple of houses down from Rory and Lauren's former family home in McBride Street, Bentleigh. The house of Jacky and his Australian wife Adele was on the corner of Searle and McBride Streets. This enabled Adele to organise *two* street parties each Christmas.

Jacky had taken retirement literally and became as retiring as Adele was outgoing. In the ensuing five years, it was common for neighbours to remark about how invisible he had become, save for Adele's annual street parties.

This was an alien concept to Rory. When he still lived at the family home, Jacky had a knack — or perhaps a method — of bumping into Rory and quickly turning the conversation to police matters. His fervent interest in murders of the day took him from being a reticent neighbourhood presence to vociferous analyst of criminality whenever he met Rory.

Not that Rory needed someone with an interest in murders — until now, that is. Jacky's qualification for the task at hand was his ability to read French and the spare time of a retiree. Jacky's former day job as a structural engineer equipped him with an ordered mind to detect relevant references and build a picture from the minutiae in Antoine Chabanne's letters. Jacky's zeal for murders would deliver the will needed to wade through the boxful of old letters.

Rory arrived unannounced and Adele answered the door. Her tone was more cautious than the welcoming manner he knew as a neighbour.

'Have you moved back?'

'No, I've actually come to visit Jacky.'

'I saw you talking to Lauren at the funeral, I thought maybe …'

'It wasn't us getting back together. Just part of life after separation … and death, I suppose.' Rory shrugged apologetically.

'What a shame. You'd better come in. Jacky will be excited to see you. He really missed chatting with you after you moved out.'

Adele took Rory through the house to a sunroom where they observed Jacky doing push-ups on the lawn.

'He's just been for a run down to the beach. It's part of his routine. Leave that box here and we'll see if he can handle breaking the regime.'

Something told Rory that Adele was more than happy to have an excuse.

'Rory! You've moved back in.' The vestiges of his accent were undetectable after forty years of living in Melbourne.

'Afraid not, Jacky,' he said accepting a vice-like hand.

Tufts of grey chest hair shone against his perpetually bronze skin. It gave Jacky's running singlet a fur-trimmed look. He reached for his glasses.

'So what brings you back to the neighbourhood?'

'You, of course. I need you to crack a case for me.'

Rory thought his flippant answer had flown over Jacky's number-one-trimmed, three-quarter head of grey hair until he answered, 'Shall we break out the white board then?'

They both laughed. Jacky noticed the cardboard archive box on the sunroom table.

'Let me make us a coffee first. One of my special double shots, Rory?'

'The real reason I came.'

'I've never been to the Rhône, my family live near Toulouse,' Jacky said after hearing Rory's account of Antoine Chabanne and Brigid O'Connell, and reading Claude Gatineau's letter.

'They didn't grow many Shiraz grapes there but the wines of Hermitage and the Rhône are known all over.'

'But you can read the letters for me?'

'I must. Wine is the blood of France,' he answered with faux pride.

'It's not such a noble request, Jacky. It probably has nothing to do with anything. Nevertheless ...' Rory paused.

'You do think it has something to do with something though?'

'More like wishful thinking to be honest Jacky. It's simply one of the shapes still to be coloured in on this picture.'

'And what will I be searching for?'

'Antoine Chabanne must have had some kind of arrangement with John Ballantyne to plant his precious vines, even if John Ballantyne only held the land under a squatter's licence. When Antoine died, his wife Brigid abandoned the vineyard and John Ballantyne appears to have returned the land to grazing. The thing that bothers me is that Antoine was a driven man who also built a substantial winery and cellar there. What undertakings would a person want from a landowner before sinking so much time and effort into an enterprise?'

'You mean, would a Frenchman's passion for making wine cause him to build on sand?'

'If you like.'

'Don't forget how important terroir has always been to French winemakers. Wine laws across the globe are based on the French notion of *appellation d'origine* — designation of origin. Good wine tastes like it comes from somewhere. So your question is partly answered in Gatineau's letter to Buvelot. Chabanne recognised a winemaking paradise where "God held a mirror to

Condrieu" — his home no less. No other land would be worthy of his vines. From that moment, his heart took over his affairs.'

'Then see if the letters tell you what decisions his heart made.'

Chapter 22

'Jesus Christ, Rory, we can afford a white board, you know.'

Inspector Richard Bourke was watching Rory Blu-Tack his tattered link diagram onto the wall of the small meeting room. The patchwork of A3 sheets needed running repairs with sticky tape to keep it in one piece.

'I was on the road when I wanted to get a handle on this.'

'You could have at least found a decent piece of paper.'

'I wouldn't wipe my arse with that,' Cockburn announced on arrival. 'Sorry I'm late. There was a prang on the Tullamarine interchange.'

'Come in, Gary. I'll get Fran to pop downstairs for coffees now that you're here. What do you guys want?'

Bourke left the room to find Fran and to allow the mood to thaw from glacial to merely frosty.

'This better not be another one of your fucking ambushes,' Cockburn hissed.

'Not my idea. This is Archie Ballantyne stuff that Bourke insisted I share.'

'Seabridge involved?'

'Looks like it.'

'Any connection to Chabanne?'

'You'll have to wait and see,' Rory said irritably, already tiring of the badgering.

'Can we begin now that the pleasantries are over?' Bourke said on his return.

'Good,' he announced, accepting their arms-folded silence as assent. 'This animosity is exactly why you're both here. The crossover on these two cases may or may not be coincidental, but I'm in danger of never knowing if you don't talk to each other. I don't want to see two results go out the window because you two refused to liaise.

'And it's not just for these two cases. Your stint in Bendigo CIU is up in three weeks,' he said, turning to Cockburn.

'Then you'll both be working together in this office again. You don't have to like each other — I lost faith in miracles at Sunday school — but I'm asking you to at least be professional.' He paused. 'No that's not right. I'm not asking, I'm telling you both. If either of you can't be professional with every person in this office, then you're no use to me. Think about it! All right?'

Rory and Cockburn lifted their heads to give feeble nods. Bourke continued.

'Rory is here to brief me about a breakthrough on the Archie Ballantyne case. Then you can tell us where you're at with Marcel Chabanne, Gary. I want us all on the same page, whether the cases are connected or not. Okay?'

Having overheard the tense preliminaries draw to a close, Fran entered and dispensed the takeaway espressos from a cardboard tray.

'Double shot long black for you Rory. Flat white Richard … and a cappuccino Gary.'

She placed the sachets of sugar on the table and left with a fourth coffee still in the cardboard holder.

'Off you go, Rory,' Bourke said as he poured sugar from its paper tube.

Rory explained about the thin ribbon of Cambrian soil that was the foundation of Heathcote's red wine reputation that emerged since the 1980s; about Antoine Chabanne and his nineteenth-century vineyard; about how Claude Gatineau showed up and gave a glowing report of Antoine's wine and a sketch of the land to the renowned Louis Buvelot; about how Seabridge came into possession of Gatineau's letter and how he used the picture to identify the land; and about Seabridge's subsequent success establishing Lady's Pass Run winery and his proposal for world domination.

'Thanks for the lesson in Australian history. Is this your special subject on Mastermind?'

'Didn't you listen to anything I said Gary?' Bourke sighed.

'Sorry,' Cockburn said.

'None of this came out until a few years after Archie Ballantyne was killed. By then, Seabridge had opened

Lady's Pass Run and bottled his first vintage. The original investigators knew that Seabridge was chasing Cambrian soil. The price had already risen with all the winegrower interest, but at the time, there was no lack of opportunities to buy the stuff. Seabridge's interest in the land was not considered out of the ordinary. After all, the deal was finalised amicably.

'What they didn't know at the time was just how badly Seabridge wanted this specific piece of land — that he must have it to the exclusion of all others.'

Rory stood up and placed a finger on the link diagram box marked "Vineyard".

'This particular parcel of land was sacred to him because it was the site of the first Shiraz grapes in the region. The provenance of that claim was captured in Gatineau's letter and drawing. Gatineau's gushing praise provided the first ever international recognition of a Heathcote Shiraz. It had the Buvelot connection that is also precious to Seabridge. It had everything. You might not have noticed when you and I met at Lady's Pass Run Gary, but the tasting room gallery is a shrine to the location. Seabridge was going to acquire that block of land no matter what, and when it appeared to have slipped from his grasp …'

'What do you mean, "slip from his grasp"? I thought the sale went through,' Bourke said.

'It did go through and Seabridge was genuinely excited about that. Enough for him to want to celebrate with Archie on the day the transaction was settled. He had courted Archie to sell the land off and on for about a year. They must have had *some* rapport.'

'So what changed?' Cockburn asked.

'He found out that the sale did not include the actual vineyard area shown in Gatineau's drawing.'

Rory explained that the land title did not include all of the fenced area that Seabridge thought he had acquired. He described how the paddock that Seabridge purchased — shown on the parish plan as one allotment — actually comprised two separate land titles. He produced a copy of the Land Victoria file note revealing that Archie discovered the discrepancy months before selling to Seabridge. It also mentioned the fifteen-year adverse possession claim process that needed to be followed to secure a Certificate of Title for the land.

Rory continued: 'When Seabridge turned up with the champagne, I reckon Archie told him that his newly acquired Certificate of Title did not include the vineyard end of the paddock. He told Seabridge he was about to fence that particular section off to retain occupancy and, over time, he would be making an adverse possession claim to acquire a freehold title. That's why he had the pile of fencing material. It was the exact amount needed for the 450-metre boundary between the two allotments.

'Archie must have been careful in his dealing with Seabridge not to promise more than eighty acres that the Certificate of Title allowed. As with all city dwellers, a big paddock is a big paddock. Seabridge wouldn't know if he was looking at eighty acres or eighty hectares. What he did know was, the thing most precious to him was slipping through his fingers.'

'You've found a motive. How do you think he killed Archie?'

Rory described Eric's theory to Bourke and Cockburn. He then added, 'It's over fourteen years since Archie was killed. Seabridge is about to become eligible to make his own adverse possession claim to secure a title for the land. I reckon his timing to begin the museum of art development is based around this opportunity.'

Rory finally took the plastic dome from its cardboard cup and sipped his cold coffee. Bourke drummed the fingers of both his hands on the table.

'Good work. I like it. But I don't see how we can make it stick.'

'He only has to plead ignorance and deny it,' Cockburn said.

'So there's no connection to Chabanne in any of this?' Bourke asked Rory.

'The Habdouds,' Cockburn answered.

'Rory?' Bourke persisted.

'I haven't found any link other than the original vineyard that Antoine Chabanne established on the same bit of land. It lasted less than twelve years because Antoine died young.'

'That's a hundred and fifty fucking years ago.'

'Nothing more recent I'm afraid,' Rory admitted.

'Well, bring him in for questioning on the Archie Ballantyne death. I'll do the interview with you. See who his lawyer mates are and see how much he sweats.'

'It'll be a pleasure,' Rory said.

'Now what about the Habdouds, Gary? Are there any other leads?'

'The Habdoud brothers both travelled to Echuca the week that Marcel Chabanne was killed, but not the father. But Mansur admitted he knew about Marcel's bird nest thing. There's no doubt they'd be up to making it look like an egg collecting accident.'

'What else have you got?'

'We're running checks on everything that will pinpoint their movements. Mobile phone calls, credit card use, tollway use and CCTV cameras. That sort of stuff. If that draws a blank, we'll start looking at who they were talking to leading up to this. We'll gather everything we can before we bring them in for official questioning.'

'And ransacking of the house?'

'I'm putting that down to opportunistic vultures. Even Rory says he's seen that happen in country towns when old-timers die. The locals expect to find money stashed in the mattress.'

'What about Seabridge. Is there anything we need to ask him about Marcel Chabanne while we have him in here?'

'There's no motive. I know Rory eventually found one for Archie Ballantyne but it'd be drawing a long bow conjuring a reason for Seabridge to kill Chabanne.'

'Rory?'

'Seabridge had the opportunity but I think we should concentrate on questioning him about Archie Ballantyne. Keep our powder dry on Chabanne in case something does show up later.'

'What fucking powder? You just can't let my case go. Can you?'

Seabridge had aimed high within his coterie of friends for legal representation. Bourke knew barrister Raymond — not Ray — from Raymond's days as a ruckman for Hawthorn and now as a player-tribunal advocate for the AFL team that Bourke barracked for. Bourke was used to Raymond espousing the ludicrousness of terms such as negligent, reckless and intentional as they were applied by the Match Review Panel to slow-motion vision of stretcher-case concussion. Raymond's success in such matters ensured a finals berth for the tribunal-prone full back who played for Raymond and Bourke's team. It stuck in Bourke's craw that he found himself on the opposite side of the table to a man he was obliged by blind team loyalty to admire. He was even more irked by the superior joviality Raymond carried into the interview room — another arena of conflict.

Seabridge sat stony-faced among the unfamiliar surroundings and the intimidating recording equipment. He only managed a half-hearted glare at Rory. Bourke pronounced the formalities before asking Rory to begin.

'As you know, we are re-investigating the death of Archie Ballantyne. New evidence has emerged that we intend to question Mr Seabridge about at this interview.'

'New evidence. My,' said Raymond.

'We've learnt that the land you purchased from Mr Ballantyne does not include the forty acres occupied by the Lady's Pass Run building and your initial vine plantings. We've also learnt that Mr Ballantyne was aware that this area was not included on the Certificate of Title. Before the sale, Mr Ballantyne received advice that he could secure a separate Certificate of Title for that particular forty acres by way of an adverse possession claim, and thereby keep the forty acres for himself. We believe that the fencing material he purchased and had on hand when you visited him was for the purpose of acting on that advice. In other words, he was going to fence off and keep the forty acres that was not included on the Certificate of Title — land that until that moment, you believed was included in the sale.'

Seabridge did not seem alarmed and turned to Raymond to respond.

'What makes you believe what Mr Ballantyne may or may not have intended to do?'

Rory handed Raymond a copy of the Land Victoria file note. He read it and passed it to Seabridge.

'Is that it?' Raymond said theatrically. 'You learnt this after fourteen years. New evidence? A formal interview? I don't see the problem. Do you have a question or did you just put us to all this trouble simply to tell us a title is missing for part of the land?'

'This constitutes a *prima facie* motive,' Bourke said with annoyance.

'So are you going to ask any questions, Inspector?'

Bourke looked at Rory.

'When did you find out that Mr Ballantyne did not have a Certificate of Title for all the land?'

Raymond nodded to Seabridge to answer.

'Archie told me about a month beforehand. He was embarrassed by it because his family had occupied the land since European settlement. But he had done his homework — as you can see by this file note. He told me that I would be able to make an adverse possession claim because the allotment he sold me held the only access to the forty acres. I've now held the land for nearly fifteen years and I'm in the throes of preparing such a claim. Raymond's firm is advising me on the matter. You know we have a mega development in advanced planning stage for the site. Securing a Certificate of Title is all part of our due diligence.'

'The file note refers to Mr Ballantyne clearly expressing a strategy to acquire a Certificate of Title for the forty acres himself,' Rory persisted.

'Archie told me that he could do so and then transfer it to me. But we both decided that would take too long and be too messy. In the end, I agreed to bear the responsibility for acquiring the Certificate of Title by adverse possession.'

'In that case, I'm surprised you're waiting the statutory fifteen years to make the claim. I understand that Mr Ballantyne's decades of exclusive rate-paying occupancy of the vineyard land is a right he could have assigned to you. With Archie's agreement, he could have provided a Deed of Assignment of Possessory Rights or even a Statutory Declaration, allowing you to lodge an adverse possession claim fourteen years ago. Surely this is the advice you would have given Mr Seabridge,' Rory said turning to Raymond.

Gleeful smugness spread across Raymond's face before he answered.

'Unfortunately, Mr Seabridge relied on Mr Ballantyne's basic understanding of the adverse possession principle. Otherwise, we would not all be sitting here wasting our time. This Land Victoria file note demonstrates the rudimentary limits of Archie's knowledge. In any case, it has only emerged as a matter Mr Seabridge needs to address since the museum of art project has been placed on the table.'

'And nothing about the forty acres was included in the contract of sale?'

'At the time I didn't imagine you could have a contract for land without title, Sergeant. I think most lay people would quickly come to that conclusion without further thought,' Seabridge said.

'It's nevertheless surprising that neither of you saw fit to take legal advice on the matter.'

'Then I'm guilty of failing to take legal advice, Sergeant. You hardly need to remind me of that.'

'And what about the fencing materials? It was the exact quantity Mr Ballantyne would need to fence the forty acres and lodge his own adverse possession claim.'

'You've already asked me about the fencing. I've no idea what Archie had in mind.'

Seabridge and Rory began a staring competition.

'Well, that's cleared that up,' Raymond said, rubbing his hands together cheerfully. 'How do you reckon our boys will go against the Hawks on Saturday, Richard? Against my old team.'

'Seabridge was more than ready for that,' Bourke said as he paced the room freshly vacated by Raymond and Seabridge. Rory remained seated and resigned.

'He's had fourteen years to get his story straight.'

'He still couldn't come up with an answer about the pile of fencing wire and posts. What does the original file say about that?'

'It's noted in the crime scene description but not anywhere else. The investigators don't seem to have regarded it as relevant — despite what Eric told them. I spoke to one of Archie's old mates in Toolleen, a neighbour called Cornell Freeman. He didn't know what Archie was up to either. Archie's wife had been dead for some years and he no longer socialised.'

'Can you find out where he bought the stuff. See if he said anything to the supplier?'

'Do you know how many providers of fencing there will be in the area? He could have got the stuff in Heathcote, Bendigo, Echuca or everywhere in between. And it was fourteen years ago, the place might not even exist anymore.'

'You're a policeman, Rory. That's what we do.'

Chapter 23

The email read:

Dear Rory,

I have completed a search for archived plans of the
Parish of Redcastle. The missing part of Crown
Allotment 56 only appears on the original sale version.
It is shown as Allotment 56A. It appears to have been
incorporated into Allotment 56 not long after. The
combined areas are drawn as one allotment on all
subsequent plans. This might have been an outcome of
the sale but there is no record documenting
amalgamation of the allotments. The absence of key
documents is not uncommon for the period, however. I
apologise for the time this has taken and hope the
information is nonetheless helpful.
Kind regards,
Fern Baillie.

Rory picked up the phone.

'Hi Fern, it's Rory James. I got your email and I'm phoning to apologise. After we met at your office I saw a copy of the original sale plan on the library's microfiche. I found out about the original Allotment 56A. I should have let you know and saved you the trouble you went to.'

'Never mind. It's interesting history ... something I like about the job.'

'I presume the allotments were amalgamated because the same person bought both of them.'

'Not necessarily ... and that wouldn't be reason enough on its own. One of my history-minded colleagues believes it may be for more sinister reasons, perhaps it was something to do with the dummying that went on at the time.'

'You mean squatters who purchased in the names of family and friends so they could exceed the purchase limit of 640 acres each year?'

'You know about that?'

'I heard about the practice from a squatter's descendant. This whole case is becoming an Australian History learning curve. It could be karma for failing the subject in year twelve.'

'They probably told you it's widely acknowledged that squatters had corrupt influence over staff at country Land Offices of the day. When they conspired to do such things, the documentation held in our files becomes scant, I'm afraid.'

'So why wasn't the Certificate of Title changed as well as the parish plan?'

'That's the biggest mystery. Perhaps the two certificates of title were retained and they simply lost one of them. Perhaps Allotment 56A still exists as a valid title. I could check with the Registrar of Titles if you like.'

'If you could, please.'

It was later the same day when she phoned.

'I got on to a friend in the Titles Office,' Fern said with eagerness. 'Allotment 56A *does* still exist as a valid title.'

'Wow,' Rory said before moderating his tone. 'That's not necessarily significant, is it?'

'No. Not if it was in the name of Ballantyne, in which case the Certificate of Title might simply have been misplaced through the generations.'

'If it's not in the name of Ballantyne, who owns it?'

'It's in the name of the original purchaser. A Brigid O'Connell, Innkeeper of Murray Road. Does that name mean anything?'

'Does a snake have hips?' Rory answered excitedly. 'She and her partner had an arrangement with Archie Ballantyne's ancestor to grow vines on this bit of dirt before it was opened for selection. Maybe Ballantyne's ancestor took advantage of that and used her as a dummy.'

'Well there's more.'

'You can't make my day any sweeter than you just did. What?'

'A title search was done for Allotment 56A about fifteen years ago. Isn't that when Archie Ballantyne sold to Seabridge?'

'So, Ballantyne would have also found out that this forty acres of land, which his family had been farming for generations, had never been held in the name of Ballantyne. It was not simply a matter of a lost title. He would have to make an adverse possession claim to acquire a valid Certificate of Title.'

'That's right.'

'Would Brigid O'Connell's descendants have a claim on the land?'

'It's hard for me to say. The amalgamation of allotments 56 and 56A suggest that it passed to Ballantyne at some stage. After such a long time, Brigid O'Connell's descendants' entitlements may have long been extinguished by Ballantyne's possession. However ...' The line went quiet as she lapsed into thought.

'What?'

'Maybe the original Certificate of Title for Allotment 56A was not surrendered at that time, in which case it could not have been extinguished for the purpose of amalgamating it with Allotment 56. That's something that even corrupt Land Office officials wouldn't have been able to overcome. And that's assuming its part of a dummying arrangement.'

'And what if someone came across the original Certificate of Title?'

'They could be sitting on a nest egg.'

Chapter 24

Nine-thirty, Thursday night in the four-poster bedroom of The Manse. Rory and Sigrid had made an early night of it. An un-early night threatened nevertheless.

'I hit a brick wall yesterday. So I came up here to do the rounds of rural suppliers. I'm knocking on shop doors trying to find someone who sold fencing materials to the victim fourteen years ago. It's what we do when things reach the desperate stage.'

'Don't you have constables to do that sort of leg work?' Sigrid asked.

'Not when you're a one man band.'

'It's not just an excuse to come back to Bendigo is it?'

'Every silver lining has a dark cloud,' Rory said as he stroked her bare thigh thoughtfully. They had recovered enough from lovemaking to be sitting in bed and drinking a third scotch.

'You're the first person I've done it with in a four-poster bed,' he mused.

Sigrid smiled at him and clinked his glass.

'So I wasn't *your* first in a four-poster bed?'

'You'd better be careful. You might end up solving the case and then where will we be,' she said to change the subject.

'There's a bit of mileage left in the case yet. I have to interrupt my quest among rural suppliers to go back to Melbourne tomorrow.'

'There are some other unsolved cases in Bendigo if you do need an excuse. Have you heard about Constable Ryan disappearing from White Hills in 1886? There's a reward of £150 if you get lucky.'

'That case sounds a bit too cold. Anyway, how come you're suddenly an expert?'

'It featured in a story in the *Bendigo Magazine*.'

She rose from the bed and padded naked to the sideboard for refills.

'Anything to stay here,' he said.

The Chabannes were already at Jacky and Adele Du Camp's house. Rory recognised the blue Golf parked in the street.

'They must be here when I tell you the tale of Antoine Chabanne,' Jacky had insisted when Rory phoned him. 'Now that I have read all the letters, I know more about Remy and Scarlet Chabanne's ancestors than they do. That is something that must be put right. I'll tell them as I tell you. The circle will no longer be broken.' His voice had risen with eagerness, 'This is something to celebrate, so Adele and I will prepare a meal we can all share.'

A waft of beguiling food smells engulfed Rory when Jacky answered the door.

'They're here already,' Rory said.

'And it's like I know them already. Antoine's story is told so intimately in his letters to his family in France. I can see his likeness in Remy.'

'No way, Jacky.'

'Scoff all you like. I know what I read and I know what I see.'

'I've brought a Heathcote Shiraz.'

Rory handed the brown paper bag to Jacky.

'Then we can compare it to the original. Remy has a Condrieu Sirah.'

The dining end of Jacky and Adele's living room was an inviting amber wash of subtle lighting and a table candelabra. Adele, Scarlet and Remy rose with their drinks from the facing lounge chairs to greet Rory.

'Bonsoir.'

'Bonsoir.'

Smiles glowed.

'Well, that's exhausted my French,' Remy joked.

'There's more French in you than you know how to speak,' Jacky told him.

'This man is wonderful Rory,' Remy said. 'He speaks to me like a psychiatrist who knows more about me than I do. Scarlet and I are so flattered that you and Adele have invited us for a meal. I can think of no better way to learn about one's family history. Thank you, Jacky and Adele.'

'It is our pleasure of course, and I know that it's a time of hurt. We should be doing this in the presence of your son and perhaps we are. Let us remember Marcel with a toast before we begin the evening. To Marcel.'

'To Marcel,' came the grave chorus of replies. Sips were taken without clinking of glasses.

Scarlet broke the solemnity. 'Thank you, Jacky. I'm pleased that you acknowledged Marcel. Let us all now enjoy the evening we have anticipated so much.'

Adele seated everyone and announced an appetizer of roasted goat cheese with honey and thyme.

'It's my Aussie version of French cooking I'm afraid.'

'It will be more authentic than the beef bourguinon I prepared for our main. Adele is the real cook in the house,' Jacky said.

'Are you all right Rory?' Adele said as she served the cheese dish to Rory. He was too choked to answer immediately. He tapped his chest as though recovering from something that went down the wrong way. Although they were all dining together for the first time, the company was already too warm and intimate for Rory to affect an excuse.

'I'm sorry. It suddenly struck me how long it's been since I sat down to a home-cooked meal with friends or family. Lauren and I separated about a year ago,' he said to Remy and Scarlet. 'This sort of reaction doesn't normally happen to me, even when I dwell on things.'

An awkward silence threatened to descend.

'Now I know our hospitality is truly valued,' Jacky responded rapidly. 'Thank you, Rory, à votre santé.'

'Santé,' came the chorus — this time with glass clinking and smiles.

It took until the main course for Rory to notice the back of a portable whiteboard in shadows at the other end of the living room.

'Is that what I think it is, Jacky? I thought you were kidding when you suggested using a whiteboard.'

'I borrowed it from my old work. It's an electronic white board. I can print off A4 copies for you. It also has several panels — they operate on rollers. I prepared all the panels before you came.'

'You didn't have to go to all that trouble.'

'Yes he did,' said Adele. 'He's an engineer.'

'A white board is perfect for this task,' Jacky defended himself. 'There are no pictures from Antoine's times so I had to gather his thoughts and descriptions into an order that tells a story. You will soon see. We will take our coffees in the lounge and I will begin. But first, Adele's pièce de rèsistance — *Épouse d'un français pavlova.*'

'Wife-of-a-Frenchman pavlova,' Adele translated.

Jacky wheeled the whiteboard in front of the lounge chairs for his seated audience of coffee drinkers. The boxes drawn in marker-pen were crammed with small writing, barely legible from the lounge chairs.

'Don't worry if you can't read it. They're mainly there as prompts for me. I can print it out for you later.'

'Did you see that our friend Cate translated a few of the letters for us? She passed away before she got very far at all.'

'Pooff,' Jacky gave the classic Gallic expression of indignation accompanied by a roll of the eyes. 'I'm sorry, but your friend Cate was obviously a non-French woman who learnt French from other non-French English speakers. She has not seen the soul in Antoine's writing. Now let me tell you about your great-great-grandfather.'

Jacky tapped the top left-hand box drawn on the white board.

'You know that Antoine sailed to Australia seeking treasure on the Victorian goldfields. However, he was in possession of treasure before he set foot on the good ship *Mathilde* at Marseilles — the Shiraz grape stems packed in moss and potato slices. The promise of these infused Antoine with fervour akin to the fever that gripped diggers on the goldfields. It blindly drove his every action until his death In a strange land.'

Adele had taken care to seat Remy and Scarlet on the two-seater lounge closest to the whiteboard. Rory joined Adele on the three-seater that was positioned to watch the television behind the whiteboard. She had patted the cushion bedside herself when Rory made for the only single armchair.

'On the *Mathilde*, Antoine learnt that as a non-British citizen he would not be able to own land. He is frank in letters to his family, telling them that he formed a priority to find a bride in whose name he could acquire land. He must have been good-looking and confident in the second French language of flirting because he writes this as something that can be taken for granted. His premiere passion is for his wine grapes. Finding a wife is a pleasure for him to savour, but nonetheless a *mariage d'utilité*.

'When did you ever learn this so-called second French language,' Adele taunted.

'Pooff. You are here, aren't you?'

Adele returned him a smile. Jacky tapped the second box drawn on the white board.

'Like me, Antoine is lucky in love. He found Brigid O'Connell almost as soon as he stepped from the ship. He is enchanted by her beauty and the soft palate of her Irish tongue. Antoine doesn't say, but I suspect it is also a *mariage d'utilité* for Brigid. When they met, she had been working in her uncle's Kilmore pub for more than a year. She has learnt the trade and had ambitions of her own. Brigid would know about the women who operated inns on the goldfield routes and on the roads to the Murray River. I suspect the desire to open an inn was more Brigid's than Antoine's.'

'You've been reading the local history too. I'm most impressed,' Rory said.

'I had to, to fill in the gaps, Rory.'

Jacky tapped the next box headed "McIvor Diggings" and continued. 'When they reached Heathcote, Antoine's priority was to plant his vines. As you already know from

Gatineau's letter, Antoine rode to the top of Mount Camel to survey the surrounding countryside for a suitable location. On the shoulder of the mountain, he discovered "God holding a mirror to Condrieu" and there was no question of planting anywhere else.

'The land was held under a squatter's licence by John Archibald Ballantyne — Archie's ancestor — who agreed to sub-lease the site to Antoine. This arrangement might not have been legally permissible at the time but it reflects the blinkered view Antoine had when it came to his vines. Brigid urged him to seek a location closer to Heathcote where small holdings of land were more likely to be opened for selection and be free of competing interest of squatters. For Antoine, the vines had already found their natural home.

'The vineyard location did however serve them well when it came to securing a site for the inn. They found land on the Murray Road, now the Northern Highway, that was close to the vines and on the flourishing coach route to Echuca and Deniliquin through Runnymede. The French rubble stone building technique enabled Antoine to erect substantial premises at little cost. The beams were hewn from trees in the adjoining Crosbie Forest and the roof was painstakingly laid with slate retrieved from mine tailings. I have not seen it, but I imagine it became a landmark the moment it was completed.

'Brigid operated the inn while Antoine dug for gold in Heathcote and tended the vines into production. Antoine and Brigid's arrival in the late 1850s was after the easy pickings of the alluvial gold rush years. Deep quartz mining had taken over in Heathcote and fortunes were less easily won by those who remained. Antoine fared better when gold was discovered at nearby Redcastle, but it was the inn that best sustained them, especially while the coach line to Echuca and Deniliquin operated.

'They both had a hand in the very productive home garden and orchard. Antoine co-opted his mining companions to excavate a tunnel into the vineyard hillside where he constructed a two-storey stone façade for the winery and cellar. There is a rough sketch of it in one of his letters. The letters translated by Cate describe this developing part of their life.

'Then comes the bit that will be of most interest to you, Rory.'

Jacky pressed a button on the electronic whiteboard. The wall of hand-written text boxes scrolled into the left-hand side of the frame and a new text-crammed panel emerged from the right.

The pleasure of being read to had settled upon them all. Jacky's gift of weaving the treads of Antoine's letters into a mesmeric story created calm anticipation. They abstained from trying to decipher the whiteboard and courteously awaited his interpretation. Scarlet held Remy's hand and Adele gave a contented smile to Rory.

'The land where Antoine planted his vines was about to come onto the market for sale. Until then, it had been Crown land held under a squatter's licence. According to the colonial history I read, the government was under pressure to release the squatters' iron grip that prevented diggers moving onto the land. The gold fields were dying and the huge population of miners were looking beyond scratching a meagre living. So, after several years of producing better and better vintages, Antoine's vineyard land became available for sale.

'The government proclaimed most of John Ballantyne's squatters run open for selection, including the vineyard block. According to Antoine, John Ballantyne intended to purchase as much of the surveyed land as he could, including the vineyard which he would continue leasing to Antoine and Brigid until they had enough money to buy it from him. Antoine also writes that John Ballantyne was a person of sufficient influence at the Land Office to have a separate forty acre allotment created specifically for the vineyard — presumably with its future sale to Antoine in mind.

'The government land sales had an annual limit of 640 acres for each purchaser, so John Ballantyne was forced to use dummies to purchase much of the land he wanted to acquire. Apparently, it was a common practice for wealthy squatters to use friends and family in this way when their runs were open for selection. Antoine was not eligible to own land but he and John Ballantyne were in cahoots to have the vineyard block purchased by Ballantyne in Brigid's name. Until then, Antoine and John Ballantyne seemed to have a trusting relationship. In his letters, Antoine refers to John Ballantyne as "*mon ami*".'

'So the Certificate of Title for the forty acre vineyard was first issued to Brigid?' Rory asked.

'The first and *only* time,' Jacky answered. 'And that's when things turned sour. Emboldened by the new freehold status of his land, John Ballantyne doubled the rent he was charging Antoine to lease the vineyard. Having paid for purchase of the land in Brigid's name, John Ballantyne also set about having it transferred into his own name. But he hadn't bargained on his dummy being anything but dumb. Despite his influence at the Land Office, he was unable to have the land transferred into his name without return of the already issued Certificate of Title. The prospect of two titles existing for one piece of land was inconceivable. Brigid dug in and refused to surrender it. In her mind, any agreement they had was voided by the outrageous rent increase.

'And that is how things stood when Antoine met his death. His last letter home is full of anguish for his vines. The site he chose had been vindicated by ever more spectacular vintages, but his vigneron utopia was threatened by a feudal-like landlord. The land of promise was suddenly one without hope.'

Remy and Scarlet sat in dispirited silence. Jacky's engrossing storytelling powers had not been able to deliver their forlorn hope of a fairy-tale ending.

'So is that how things sat — Antoine dead, the vineyard abandoned and Brigid holding the Certificate of Title?'

'Not quite, Rory. There is one last letter — this time from Brigid.'

'I've never noticed a letter in English,' Scarlet said.

'No. She wrote it in English of course. But the Chabannes of Condrieu had to have it translated. It is in a different hand to Antoine's. The English original was not kept. This is what it said.'

Jacky pressed the electronic whiteboard button to reveal its third and last panel. Jacky had translated the copy of Brigid's letter back into English and transcribed it onto the whiteboard. Rory, Adele, Remy and Scarlet read:

Dear Monsieur and Madame Chabanne,

The painful task has fallen upon me of disclosing to you the death of your gallant and greatly lamented son Antoine. He died by falling from a prohibitive height and broke his neck. I know it will be of meagre comfort to you but he fell from the parapet of the winery that he built. It was there or amongst his vines from Condrieu that he was never happier in this distant land.

I hope Antoine has told you in his letters that he and myself chose some years ago to be together, although we had not yet blessed our union in marriage. It has been as a devoted couple that we have made our home and our enterprise in this fine country. From our combined industry, our roadside inn and the vineyard and winery have risen to sustain our earthly needs. Until Antoine's death, seldom did we suffer a poor day in our endeavours. I must be careful not to cast aspersions but Antoine's and my own wont to secure the vineyard land has seen us at harsh odds with the landlord who held licence to the land. We have seen his benevolence fade along with his accord to sell the property to Antoine and me. His wrath has been aroused by our withdrawal from his scheme to acquire freehold ownership of the land in the first instance. I know that Antoine has told you about these contrivances in his letters to you. As it now sits, I am most fearful that the vines from Condrieu will wither.

If this intrigue has caused any other hand to have played a part in Antoine's death, then sleep well in the knowledge that the title to the soil where the vines of Condrieu grow will not pass to another. It is my silent vow to Antoine that ownership of the soil shall remain forever beyond the reach of all others. I do be thinking of the great sorrow my letter carries but i can tell you also that I bear Antoine's child. The babe will be born in the spring of this hemisphere and I have resolved to name it Antoine if it be a boy and Antoinette if it be a girl. Although the infant will not know its father, it shall be proudly honoured with his family name.

I must now conclude by wishing a sad adieu.

Respectfully yours,
Brigid O'Connell.

'It was a boy,' Remy said quietly. 'Antoine Chabanne was the first in the family to do law at Melbourne University.'

After the Chabannes' departure, Adele bid goodnight and left Jacky and Rory to enjoy scotch nightcaps in the lounge chairs of the snug. Jacky topped up their glasses.

'I better take a taxi home tonight,' Rory said.

'It's a shame you're not still living in your old house.'

'Every house, every front fence and every tree in the street reminded me of that when I arrived tonight.'

'Sorry, Rory.'

Rory gave a nonchalant shrug. They leant back in mellow contemplation of the night's disclosures.

'So has Brigid succeeded in preventing ownership of the vineyard by anyone else?' Jacky asked.

'Amazing as it seems after a hundred and fifty years, I think she has. No one seems to have the original title to the land that was issued in her name.'

'Then what a woman. To Brigid O'Connell.'

Jacky leant over to clink his tumbler with Rory's.

'And what about the Lady's Pass Run? Don't they have a title for the land it sits on? The situation must have been dealt with somehow.'

'Apparently not. It seems that the vineyard end of the paddock passed to Lady's Pass Run without a title for the land. However, they have possession and there is a process to acquire property occupied without challenge for fifteen years. A new title will then be issued.'

'Fifteen years. How long ago did that other bloke die?'

'You mean Archie Ballantyne?'

'Yeah. Isn't that when the Lady's Pass Run began?'

'Hang on, Jacky. You're trying to join a lot of dots there.'

'And you're not?'

'Well maybe I am, but I'm not supposed to share that information.'

'Well, there's nothing stopping me sharing my information. Let me tell you what I think.'

'I'm all ears,' Rory said, giving a knowing salute with his glass.

'I don't know anything about Archie Ballantyne, but what if Marcel found the Certificate of Title? He's been living in Brigid's house for a while. It sounds like she would have stashed it well, in which case it would not be easily found. But someone living in Brigid's house for a period of time … maintaining the place with a bit of work here and there. Surely it's only a matter of time before they come across it.'

Jacky paused.

'You're not saying no,' he said.

'Someone ransacked the place after Marcel died.'

'Well, there you have it. Marcel found the land title, the Lady's Pass Run bloke finds out about it and kills Marcel. Then searches for the title so he can destroy it. Voilà!'

'My only problem Poirot, is that the supposition is useless unless I have that title.'

'Poirot was a Belgian, not French,' Jacky said indignantly. 'But tell me Sherlock, do you know if the ransacker found what they were after?'

'Touché,' Rory acknowledged with a raised glass. 'I didn't know about the title when I discovered the ransacking. Whoever did it extended their search into the outbuilding and beyond. So I don't think they found it. There were too many stones overturned without result.'

'Then that must be your grail.'

'The title might not be in the house. The ransacker did a pretty thorough job. Even the skirting boards and architraves were lifted.'

'Did they dig the ground?'

'No … but there would have been freshly-turned soil somewhere if that's where Marcel unearthed it in the first place … literally.'

They resumed their mellow contemplation, perusing the golden liquid in their tumblers for inspiration.

'Then perhaps you are not aiming high enough,' Jacky decided. 'Marcel was an egg collector. He could climb.'

'You think he put it in a nest?'

'Maybe. Maybe in a tree hollow where the parrots nest.'

'If that's the case, he's probably succeeded in doing what Brigid did. It will be lost for another 150 years.'

'You're not going to give up are you?'

'I'll go back and do my own search, but …'

Jacky's brow creased in the ensuing late-night-third-scotch conversation pause.

'Don't worry Jacky. This is not the end of it. The stuff you did translating those letters was great. It fills in a lot more blanks. Helps us build a bigger picture. I like the way you presented it on the electronic whiteboard. Where did you get that?'

His face un-creased with the praise.

'Like I said, I borrowed it from my former work. By the time I retired, we couldn't workshop projects without one of those. Much better than the days of blackboards and chalk.'

Rory's eyes widened and his body stiffened back into life.

'Chalk! That's it.'

'What?' Jacky said, glancing around the room as if someone else had entered to join the conversation.

'I reckon I know where to look. Do you know how to use a cherry picker?'

'Of course. We used them all the time to do close up inspections of overpasses and bridges. Cracks in concrete and that sort of thing. I have an operator's licence.'

'Then how would you like to come with me to "the miniature France distant from France"?'

Chapter 25

Jacky arrived towing the platform lift in a trailer behind his silver Nissan Patrol. The bright green folded boom arm was emblazoned with the name Bandit Lift Hire, their phone number and logo — a Beagle Boys cartoon-style mask.

'Of all the companies to hire from for a police job,' Rory greeted him.

'I needed someone with a Niftylift HR12 … my favourite portable cherry picker model,' he said to Rory. 'Where would you like it?'

'The chalk marks were on this end,' Rory answered as he stood at the end of the forecourt with a view of the front and one end of the coaching house. 'The marks have disappeared with the rain we've had in the meantime. I'll get my camera and check the photos I took.'

They were soon standing in the shade of the entrance squinting at the small LCD screen on the back of Rory's camera.

'I should have printed it out. I think that's a chalk mark, just right of centre and I think I remember one beside that small window below the eave.'

The tiny arched window sat immediately below a small gabled hip at the end of the main roof gable. It was the only window on the entire end wall of stone.

'I wouldn't be able to see chalk marks on that, even if I had my glasses. Why don't I set the cherry picker up and start looking at the real thing?'

'That's what we're here for.'

'Did you tell Remy what we are up to?'

'"More crime scene investigation," I said. But I think he knows we're probably looking for the vineyard land title … especially when I asked him not to tell Cockburn. That's who's dealing with Marcel's murder. My bailiwick is strictly cold cases, Archie Ballantyne in particular.'

'Will this have anything to do with Archie Ballantyne?'

'I have my suspicions.'

'Then surely this is legitimate. Why can't you work together?'

'You haven't met Cockburn.'

'Well let's find the document and then it will all be academic.'

'Not even then, Jacky. That's when my work will really begin.'

'We pay you blokes with our taxes, you know.'

'It makes me despair too, Jacky. Let's just see if we can find this thing. It's still a long shot.'

Jacky clambered into the cherry picker basket and manoeuvred the unit down the trailer ramps. He positioned it at the end of the coaching house.

'You coming up?' he asked Rory.

'Can it take two?'

'What do you weigh?'

'Ninety kilos.'

'Then we'll be well under the weight limit.'

'Won't you need to have an observer down here?'

'Are you afraid of heights?

'It's a long way up there,' Rory said with a face full of unease.

'You're off the hook. I only have one harness. And I *do* need you on the ground to direct me.'

'You bastard.'

Jacky wiggled into his harness, still smiling to himself.

'Just to the right of the gable window,' Rory yelled, glancing between his camera's LCD screen and the slow whirring ascent of Jacky.

'What am I looking for?' Jacky called when he positioned himself six metres up and within reach of the tiny arched window of fixed glass.

'He would need something strong and grip-able for one hand so his other hand was free to stash whatever the document was held in. Is there any sign of someone gripping the eaves or the window surround?'

'Nothing that has displaced years of dust grime. I'll follow the eave line.'

The cherry picker whirred to life and Jacky followed the gable eave across the end of the coaching house and returned to the original position by the window.

'Anything?' Rory called.

'Nothing obvious. The roof slates are too unstable to grab. Let me see if he could get his fingers under this barge board.'

Jacky felt under the weathered facia plank that covered the line where the stone wall met the eave.

'It's a bit loose. You can squeeze your hand under it and onto the top stones.'

'So if you were hanging by one arm there, where could you reach to stash something?'

Jacky kept his left hand holding on to rock beneath the facia board and reached here and there with his right arm — like a blind man feeling for a cupboard door handle.

'He'd be too low to get it under a roof slate … Hang on, what's this?'

'What?'

'One of the stones is loose. Look.'

Jacky turned from the wall to face Rory with a stone the size of a half brick.

'I'll manoeuvre over to have a look in.'

The cherry picker's electric motor whirred. Rory could see Jacky with his forearm in the gap where the rock had come from.

'*Qu'est-ce que c'est que ça?*'

'What?'

Jacky turned in the work platform to look down to Rory. This time he held a leather tube.

'*Fantastique!*' Rory yelled.

Rory couldn't believe how slowly the cherry picker descended the six metres. *Is this the longest one minute and twenty seconds of my life?* he wondered.

The container was crafted from thick red cowhide into a tube about eight centimetres in diameter. A base plate of leather was sewn into one end and a long, fitted leather cap slid over the other. The cap was fastened with a buckle. The leather, although mottled by the heat and cold of one hundred and fifty seasons, had recently been brought back to glowing life with beeswax.

'Aren't you going to open it?' Jacky said as he watched Rory hold it, feel it, and contemplate it with reverence.

'Yeah,' he said quietly.

He unfastened the buckle and slid off the cap, noting how snugly it still fitted. He turned the opening to Jacky to show him that it contained a document.

'Help me with this will you? I don't want to put prints on the document.'

They worked on the bonnet of Jacky's Nissan Patrol to slide the Certificate of Title from the tube, unroll it and place it into a clear plastic sleeve.

The Certificate of Title for Crown Allotment 56A was the pigeon pair to Patrick Seabridge's title for Crown Allotment 56. The same coat of arms with the lion and a unicorn. The gothic heading of "Certificate of Title". The name was different of course — *Brigid Mary O'Connell of Murray Road Mount Camel, Inn keeper, is now the proprietor of ...* — as was the red shape of the land drawn on the lower left-hand side of the document. But the north side measurement of 2224 links matched perfectly with the south side boundary shown on Patrick Seabridge's title.

'Is this the missing piece in your puzzle?' Jacky asked.

'In more ways than one.'

'Then now what?'

'We celebrate. Let me take you to lunch at Cellar and Store in Heathcote. But we have to go via Redcastle. I have a book to return.'

They arrived unannounced in a convoy of two at Redcastle Creek homestead. There was no creeping up on Marjorie Goodwell however; she was waiting on the veranda steps.

'I've brought your book back,' Rory told her after introducing Jacky. 'I got through it and I can see why you were compelled to get those stories down on paper. The Goodwell's determination and achievements are impressive.'

'Thank you, Rory. Can I make some tea for you and Jacky?'

'Thanks all the same, but we're heading into town for lunch. I presume you weren't able to find out how Antoine Chabanne met his death.'

'Didn't you get my message?' she said.

'What message?'

'I found what you wanted in the newspaper archives. I phoned and left a message. Not on your number though — I don't know what I did with that. I phoned the Bendigo police station and they put me through to Sergeant Cockburn. He said he'd pass it on to you. That was weeks ago.'

'What the fuck are you doing here?'

'Your usual greeting,' Rory said.

'Well?' Cockburn leant back in his office chair where Rory had found him online at his workstation in Bendigo police station.

'I've come for my message from Marjorie Goodwell.'

'That old bat. She's a nutcase. She phoned you about one of the Chabannes dying in the nineteenth century. That's two centuries before the one we're in now. Two centuries,' he repeated for emphasis. 'I know you do cold cases but that is ridicu-fucking-lous. What's next on your list? Who killed the Pharaoh Tutankhamun?'

'There is a link.'

'Link my fucking arse. You know what I think? I think you're digging up whatever shit you can just to have an excuse to come to Bendigo and root Sigrid Dobell.'

Rory leant down to Cockburn's face and said with measured fierceness, 'Listen dickbrain. I'm this far away from walking out of here with the truth about Marcel Chabanne's death. In fact that's just what I'm going to do,' he decided straightening up. 'I'll do this with Bourke instead so he can see just how well you have fucked this up … again.'

Rory was in the car park before Cockburn reached him.

'Okay country boy, keep your Akubra on.'

Rory gave him the ray.

'I'm not gonna say I'm sorry. Half the blokes in this station would fancy the opportunity to root Sigrid Dobell.'

Rory turned and pressed a button on the car key. The indicators blinked to the sound of the lock clunking open.

'All right. I won't mention Sigrid Dobell. But don't forget Chabanne is my case and Bourke banged *both* our heads together, not just mine. Do you wanna be the first to run to mummy?'

Rory glared.

'Well?' insisted Cockburn.

Rory clicked the "close" button and the car blinked again.

'Did you get anything on the Habdouds?'

'Eugene and Stephen and the old man all have alibis. We're working through their recent contacts to see who else they would have used.'

'You're wasting your time. Seabridge did it.'

'How? Why?'

Rory leant back against the Commodore and told Cockburn how and why.

'It just gets better doesn't it? Your own version of *Treasure Island* and *Indiana Jones*. I remember when you were a real copper.'

'The Certificate of Title is genuine.'

'You've already been through this with Seabridge about his transaction with Ballantyne. He denied it in a flash and you had nowhere to go. You were lucky he didn't take the matter further.'

'This is different. He's now on the brink of something far bigger. It's not just the resort development itself. He's got half the arty end of Melbourne involved as investors or on the advisory board of his proposed museum of art. Do you think he's going to sit on his hands if Marcel shows up claiming ownership of the land?'

'Just because you found the land title doesn't mean Chabanne approached Seabridge with it. As it stands, you've got less than what you fronted him with about Ballantyne.'

'I haven't given up on him killing Archie Ballantyne either. A lot of stuff on the original file can be viewed differently now we have a motive. You think about that — people have dreams that they strive for and they may or may not achieve them. But this bloke has been in the position of reaching his prize, reached that moment when he thinks it's safe enough to relax his guard and give an inner fist clenching "Yes!", and then he has it ripped completely and unexpectedly from his grasp by Archie

Ballantyne. And what if that happens to him again after a fourteen year wait to put things right? A word probably hasn't been invented to describe that feeling — he had to act.'

'He denied one. Why give him the chance to deny a second?'

'Why not rattle his cage in any case? See how he reacts when we tell him that a separate title actually exists; that we found that title; that the title is in Brigid O'Connell's name. Can't you see the significance of that in Seabridge's world? On the face of it, the land is no longer his. Aren't you remotely curious about how he takes the news? If he was hearing about it for the first time, you'd expect every drop of blood to drain from his face. My bet is he won't flinch.'

Cockburn was answerless.

Rory persisted.

'You're going to have to tell him about the title showing up in any case. That's before you hand it back to Remy and Scarlet Chabanne. He won't be too pleased about that bit either.'

Cockburn rubbed his hands over the bristles on his scalp.

'All right. All right. We'll do it. But you do the talking. I'll be recording proceedings. If this thing fucks up, I'm gonna have proof that it's squarely on your head.'

Chapter 26

'There,' Cockburn said and pointed ahead of the tram. A vertical blue fabric banner above the shop veranda read "SEABRIDGES". It was fixed tautly between horizontal rods protruding between the two upstairs windows of the High Street shop.

Cockburn and Rory made their way to the middle doors of the tram, ready to alight at the next stop. The ticket inspector version of Cockburn faced Cockburn.

'I didn't see you validate a ticket.'

'It wouldn't fit,' Cockburn said and held his police badge too close to the inspector's nose for him to read the motto "Uphold the Right".

'Fucking Malvern,' Cockburn said as if the suburb's existence was somehow responsible for the tram company hiring someone of his own disposition.

'What are you gonna do if you ever have to be the good cop?' Rory asked.

'Whoever I'm with will have to fake being badder than me.'

'Christ, you've already considered the possibility.'

'Just don't fuck up this Seabridge thing.'

Up close, the shop veranda was a fashionable black canvas awning. Panels either side and below the shop windows were also in a hip black finish. The worn chrome-plated glass frames and the tessellated tiles on the doorway alcove however betrayed the original early-twentieth-century construction. Gold leaf lettering beside the door was also a nod to the past.

SEABRIDGE ART DEALERS
Open - Tuesday to Friday 11AM to 6PM,
Saturday 11AM to 4PM, or by appointment.
Sales – Appraisals and valuations – Art rental – Consultancy

It was the same story inside — new gallery up to ceiling height where the original plaster ceiling lurked in the shadows of the high-tech lighting and suspended panels. The hidden deco cornices were fragmented where walls had been removed to create the free space of the gallery.

Ursula Ryman was standing behind a blade thin woman seated at a white table. The clean desk policy allowed only a cordless phone and a white laptop that they both gazed at intently. Rory marvelled at how well Ursula could wear a plain white shirt.

'Sergeant James. Is there a problem?' she said, glancing at Rory, then Cockburn and then the briefcase that Rory held.

'We need to update Patrick about a development affecting the Lady's Pass Run land.'

'Oh.' Her face stilled as questions rushed into her mind. None reached her lips.

'He's upstairs. I'll take you up.'

An electronically locked glass door that Rory hadn't noticed led up an enclosed stairwell that served as an extension of the gallery — more polished wood and white walls. Aboriginal dot paintings marked their ascent until they reached the first-floor display cum meeting cum entertaining space. Its tall windows overlooked the tram cables of High Street. Contemporary canvases hung beside the meeting table. Rory recognised a small urban study by Jeffrey Smart.

Ursula swiped her electronic key card on the white rear door to disclose a warren of miscellany underpinning the gallery's simplicity. A room to the left housed a computer server and security control rack with blinking lights and several CCTV screens. Beyond that was a long narrow office with two PCs along a bench. Seabridge was visible on the phone, navigating by mouse as he spoke. An alcove beyond the office housed a wide framing bench. The rest of the back-of–house space was tightly packed from floor to ceiling with storage. A small kitchen jutted from the back wall.

Ursula tapped on the glass and they watched Seabridge compute their presence. Without taking the handpiece from his ear, he signalled two minutes and pointed to the front room. She led them back to the entertaining space.

'Would you like a drink?' Ursula asked as Rory homed in to admire the Jeffrey Smart. Cockburn stood at the window watching the traffic below.

'A black tea would be nice.'

'Plain water,' Cockburn said.

'You look a bit taken by the Jeffrey Smart, Sergeant James.'

'I never expected to see one so small.'

'Less than $5,000 if you're interested.'

'Not right now, thanks all the same,' he said. The back-of-house door lock clicked open and she left to make the teas.

'She'll tell him that it's about the land,' Cockburn said.

'Good. We don't want him to think we're here about a murder.'

'I'll leave you to it,' Ursula said, having dispensed the drinks from a tray. She headed down the stairs as Seabridge joined them at the table.

'I believe you have some news for me, gentlemen,' he said, holding the saucer and lifting his teacup to sip.

'We do have some important news about the Lady's Pass Run land. Sergeant Cockburn would like to record what I say to make sure that what I tell you is not misleading in any way — in a legal sense.'

Cockburn placed a mobile-phone size recorder on the table.

'Should I have Raymond here?'

'You'll probably want to consult a property lawyer after our discussion.'

'Can you just tell me what's going on then?'

'We've come into possession of the Certificate of Title for the Lady's Pass Run vineyard land.'

'Oh.'

Seabridge dropped his eyes to the bare table before him. A faint tram ding filled the pregnant interval.

'You mean the piece for which we intend to submit an adverse possession claim?'

'Yes.'

Only the fainter hum of traffic intruded on the lengthening lull.

'Where did you find it?'

'I didn't say we found it, I said it came into our possession.'

'Of course. Have they said what they intend to do with it?'

'Who are you assuming the "they" are and why are you worried they might intend to do something with it?'

'What are you getting at?'

'I expected that someone who is missing a title for their land would be overjoyed when it turns up. It could spare them the trouble and cost of making an adverse possession claim.'

Seabridge looked incredulously at Rory.

'You're not telling me you have the title to the land and it's in Archie Ballantyne's name are you?'

'No. I was curious about your reaction. The title is in the name of Brigid O'Connell.'

'And do the Chabannes know?'

'They know that the land was originally purchased in Brigid O'Connell's name as a dummy for Archie's squatter ancestor,' Rory said. 'But I don't think any of this is news to you.'

Rory had snapped the fasteners of his briefcase. He reached in and produced a photocopy of the Certificate of Title before Seabridge could respond. Seabridge glanced at it and looked at Rory and Cockburn.

'What would happen if the Chabannes asserted ownership of the land?' Cockburn asked.

Rory looked with surprise at Cockburn.

'You know as well as I do what is at risk for me,' Seabridge answered.

Rory looked at Cockburn who gave him a *back to you* nod.

'You seem far more surprised that the title has been unearthed than by whose name the title is in. Is that because you've seen it recently?'

'Of course not. If I had the title I'd …'

Rory gave him time to finish his thought. When it was obvious it would not be forthcoming, Rory said, 'That's right. Surely the first thought of anyone in your position who came across this Certificate of Title would be to burn it. It threatened your adverse possession claim, your vineyard, your art museum development, your credibility. Life as you know it.'

'Ridiculous! *You* have the title. I can't possibly have been tempted in the way you say.'

'But in what other way could you have been tempted.'

'What do you mean?'

'We believe Marcel Chabanne located the title before he died. Did he come to you about it?'

'Of course not. Otherwise, it's something I would have dealt with him about.'

'Are you sure? You haven't seemed surprised that the title exists and is in Brigid O'Connell's name. We also believe that whoever ransacked the coaching house after Marcel's death, was looking for the title.'

'I've just said to you, if Marcel came to me with this I would have sorted it out with him. I certainly knew him well enough. Even if the legalities were not straightforward, it doesn't mean they were insurmountable ... or that things were more in his favour than mine. This is simply a legal situation. Isn't that why you said you're here?'

'It sounds like you've already given it some thought,' Cockburn chipped in.

'What if Marcel expressed greater expectations to you about the land title being in his family's name?' Rory persisted.

The sharper questions caused Seabridge's façade of barely concealed tolerance to crack. The pushed-up chin and chillingly raised eyelids re-surfaced.

'I read that you're treating Marcel's death as suspicious so I suppose this is just another one of your fishing expeditions. It was offensive enough when you tried it on about Archie Ballantyne. You've delivered your message about the title. As you say, it's a matter for me to deal with my lawyers about — along with a little matter of undue harassment. Don't think this is the end of this little interlude.'

He stood to conclude the discussion. Cockburn was quick to follow suit. Rory leant back in his chair to address Seabridge. 'You said the alpacas shat everywhere and stank because they don't travel well.'

Cockburn and Seabridge looked stunned and turned to each other with an expression that said, "It beats me what he's talking about".

Rory continued, 'That's what you told Sergeant Cockburn and me when you took us to Marcel's body. You said you cleaned your Hilux before setting off to get firewood because the alpacas you collected the day before shat all over it.'

'What's that got to do with any of this?'

'Alpacas are never washed, and they still don't smell. Their dung doesn't even have an odour. That's right. At least *they* can claim their shit doesn't stink. And they travel without fuss. In fact, they will wait hours in a vehicle before relieving themselves.'

'Your animal husbandry knowledge is fascinating Sergeant. I nevertheless cleaned the ute. So what?'

'Marcel Chabanne lost a heap of blood wherever he actually fell. I think whoever transported his body to the forest would have a lot of blood to clean up in their vehicle.'

Seabridge shifted on his feet. 'Stop this now. If you think I killed Marcel you had better get some evidence and then go through whatever process you have, which is not going to happen in any case because none of this happened in real life.'

'Evidence like this,' Rory said and opened his briefcase again. He placed a clear plastic bag on the table with some clothes inside.

'These are the clothes Marcel was wearing. See these fine chocolate brown hairs?' Rory pointed to a spot in the plastic bag as he held it closer to Seabridge in his other palm. 'I reckon the crime scene analysts will be able to match those with the chocolate brown alpaca at Lady's Pass Run. I understand Constable Caiden Logan is parked at the Lady's Pass Run gate waiting to take the crime scene investigators to the alpaca paddock the moment I phone him.'

Seabridge sat down.

'I also noticed the gravel repair patches below the parapet of the winery façade. The crime scene crew will be excavating below there to see how far down the traces of Marcel's missing blood loss reached. Did you know that is also the exact place Antoine Chabanne fell to his death?'

Cockburn fought not to say anything as Seabridge held his cheeks and looked to the ceiling in a collecting-his-thoughts kind of way. At length, he inhaled deeply and lowered his voice to impart well-practised gravity.

'I'm not going to respond to that. You come here about a missing land title and use the meeting as an ambush. You told me I don't need a lawyer and you have a tape recorder running. I don't think this is worthy of continuing.'

His lips had a tightness that few of his friends and enemies would recognise.

'Perhaps we have digressed a bit,' Rory said with goading cheerfulness. 'Now might be a good time to call Raymond. I think Sergeant Cockburn would like to move on to a formal interview. We'll arrange for a car to come and take us all to the station.'

'Fucking alpaca shit. You country boys sure have fascinating hobbies,' Cockburn said as they waited on the street for the police car to arrive.

'I Googled it,' Rory said.

'You know Constable Logan is on leave this week?'

'Oh, did I misunderstand what you told me?'

'What do you mean misunderstood? We never had a conversation about Caiden Logan or any other uniform.'

'Then you'd better get someone out to Lady's Pass Run to deal with the crime scene stuff — round up that alpaca. And here're Marcel's clothes, you'll need to get them submitted as evidence,' he said, handing Cockburn the brief case.

'Where did you dig these up? Didn't you say the Bendigo morgue threw them out?'

'I remember telling you his clothes were in their rubbish skip.'

'And what are you gonna pluck out of your arse for Archie Ballantyne's murder?'

'I'm working on it.'

Chapter 27

'It's beautiful,' Scarlet Chabanne said.

Her willowy fingers held the leather document holder like a jeweller displaying a necklace.

'We discovered where Marcel must have found it in the wall cavity when he began renovating the bathroom. It was behind the original lining, so the last person to handle it before Marcel would have been Brigid.'

'She must have passed her sentiments with it. If only he had brought it to Remy and me.'

There was no answer Rory could give.

'Remy will love this,' Scarlet said, renewing her inspection of the leatherwork. 'It must have stiffened to a crisp before Marcel found it. He's done a beautiful job bringing it back to life with beeswax.'

'The important thing is that it remained tightly sealed for all that time.'

'Amazing,' she said and began unbuckling the lid.

'Here's a copy of the Certificate of Title. We'll be able to give you the original after it's been used as evidence in the trial.'

Rory handed her the copy Certificate of Title in a protective plastic sleeve.

'Remy will love this too. He won't want to part with the real document if we sell the land. It seems related to the family as much as the land itself.'

'Is he working late? I thought I might catch you both at home.'

'Remy has thrown himself into his work more than ever since Marcel died.'

'I guess we all cope differently.'

Awkwardness threatened and Rory added, 'Did you say you were going to sell the land?'

'We'll sell whatever of Seabridge's vineyard land we end up with. Remy and I could never walk across the winery's threshold where Marcel and Antoine died.'

'You make it sound like there is doubt about your ownership.'

'Resurrecting the dormant title creates a murky situation, especially now the land has substantial improvements on it. We suspect our entitlement will be challenged. Then there's the matter of past wills and probates that may or may not apply. On top of all that, if Seabridge is convicted of Archie's murder, the proceeds of crime regulations might kick in. Do you know anything about that?'

'It's not my area of expertise I'm afraid. But you're lucky, you're married to a lawyer.' Rory instantly regretted using the word "lucky".

'It's so complex, Remy is taking advice outside his own legal practice. Nevertheless, we would still like to see Lady's Pass Run survive. It is after all a tribute to Antoine's original vision.'

'It'll be a shame if it doesn't. I was as seduced by Antoine's story as much as Patrick Seabridge was. It must be inspiring to be connected to those long un-told beginnings of Shiraz growing on Australian Cambrian soil.'

'Oh, but the telling has also unearthed deeper links to the home of Shiraz on the Rhône. We will always have that in the family. And like Antoine, we're ready to discover new lands, even at this time of life. We've bought a block overlooking Apollo Bay.'

'But what about the coaching house?'

'We're selling that too. With what has happened, we can't bring ourselves to scatter Marcel's ashes there.' She didn't let Rory dwell on the thought and held up the document holder. 'Perhaps we can place this in the bathroom wall cavity of the place we build at Apollo Bay — behind a pane of glass this time.'

'Have you placed the coaching house on the market yet?'

'There was no need. We already have a buyer. I phoned Mr Habdoud.'

'Mansur Habdoud?' Rory repeated, pulling a face full of distaste and disbelief.

Scarlet managed a soft smile at his bemusement.

'Yes. He wasn't home when I rang so I spoke to his wife Rashida and told her. She was ecstatic. She and her daughter Nina set off to buy curtains that day.'

'You know, Mansur was actually desperate not to buy the coaching house. He was only going through the motions to keep Rashida and Nina happy. He thinks it is a peasant house. If he gets his hands on it, he'll put cladding over the stone, fit aluminium windows and concrete the garden — that's if he doesn't bulldoze it all.'

'I know, but Rashida told me she won't let him. She gets what the place is about. Rashida is going to buy it in her own name for Nina. The coaching house began life with a female owner running a café of sorts. Perhaps there's another strong-willed woman for Marjorie Goodwell to include in her *Ladies of Lady's Pass.*'

Chapter 28

'Look at you in another new suit and tie. Remember the first night you came back to The Manse? You looked like a middle-aged goth-gone-wrong in your tattered suit and miserable face. What a mess you were in.'

'Yeah, well.'

'Hey, don't give me that face again. That was then. This is now,' Sigrid scolded. 'What's in the bag?'

'Food,' Rory said. 'I'm going to cook tonight. Fancy a stir-fry?'

'I thought we'd be at the Whirrakee, celebrating getting the case to court. Aren't you on expenses? Like when we first met — you being paid to come and stay with me?'

'Like a gigolo?'

'What's the going rate then?' she smiled.

'A bottle of Shiraz for a start. I can't prepare without a wine in my hand. And have you got an apron?'

'How did the first day in court go?' she asked when they settled down in the kitchen. Sigrid on a stool at the bench top, Rory chopping onion.

'It's a done deal. Going through the motions stuff.'

'Really?' she said with faux suspicion. 'New suit. Haircut. Were the jury impressed?'

'We still have to make sure the defence doesn't pull a swiftie.'

'But *The Age* says Patrick Seabridge is going to plead guilty.'

'The prosecutor's office did a deal to drop the charge of murdering Archie Ballantyne if he pleaded guilty to the manslaughter of Marcel Chabanne.'

'How can throwing somebody off a two-storey wall be manslaughter?'

'They argue it was not premeditated. According to Seabridge, Marcel initially fronted him *without* the Certificate of Title. He told Seabridge that he wanted to restore what he reckoned rightfully belonged to the Chabanne family. Seabridge told him to piss off. He allegedly told Marcel he didn't believe the title existed or that it was ever in Marcel's family name.'

'Allegedly? You're not in the witness box now.'

'Force of habit,' Rory apologised, knife paused above the steak. 'Anyway, Marcel allegedly … sorry. According to Seabridge, Marcel rode his bike back the next day with a photocopy. Seabridge had just released the two alpacas into the top yard and was walking down the path across the winery façade. That's how he reckons they ended up meeting at that exact spot. Seabridge's story is that he tore up the photocopy. Watching the bits flutter over the steep drop was too much for Marcel. He shoved Seabridge in the chest. Seabridge said he instinctively shoved back. He told the jury that the drop behind Marcel only entered his mind as Marcel kept falling away from him. When you spin a story like that, and there's no one who can verify or challenge it, you get off with manslaughter.'

'You think something more pre-meditated happened?'

'I don't reckon an opportunity would have presented itself so easily. He's capable of a cold-blooded action. There was more than a bit of thought put into killing Archie Ballantyne, even if it was hasty.'

'So why did they drop the Archie Ballantyne charge? Is Seabridge untouchable?'

'I don't know. He is well off and well represented though.'

'But it's murder.'

'The motive for killing Ballantyne may have been strong, but the evidence was weak. Even if Archie *was* going to use the pile of fencing material to retain the vineyard land, it doesn't necessarily incriminate Seabridge. The only real bit of new evidence was from a bloke on a tractor ploughing a paddock. He was one of the original witnesses who spotted the smoke across the countryside. It was his statement that fixed the time of the fire. Anyway, when I re-questioned him, he reckons he saw Seabridge driving to Archie's place more than forty minutes before the fire. In the original investigation, no one thought to ask him about anything other than the smoke. He didn't think anything else was important.'

'It all sounds open and shut to me.'

'He's in his seventies now, and he's recalling something that he saw from a fair distance fourteen years ago. They'd have him doubting his own name if he was ever cross-examined.'

'Aren't you disappointed?'

'It sticks in my craw. The worst thing about trading off the Archie Ballantyne case is losing the opportunity to do Seabridge on the proceeds of crime. The Lady's Pass Run was built on that murder.'

'Won't the Chabannes' claim on the land bring his empire down anyway?'

'The art museum was dead in the water the moment Seabridge was charged. Of course his own life was ruined too, but he might want to keep the winery going to re-badge it and re-invent himself whenever he gets out. The Chabannes intend selling any entitlement that comes their way, although I can't see them selling to Seabridge. I know they'd like to see the winery continue as a tribute to Antoine, but not at any cost. My guess is they'll only sell if Seabridge sells his interest. That way they can get a new owner in to honour Antoine's Shiraz legacy with dignity and free of stigma.'

'Maybe we could take it on?'

'Ha!'

'What do you mean? I made a go of this place, didn't I? We could do accommodation at the Lady's Pass Run — sub-lease the winery.'

'You know what happened last time the place was sub-let? That's how Antoine Chabanne came to grief.'

'At the hand of Archie's ancestor?'

'That's what Brigid O'Connell inferred in her letter. John Ballantyne is another one who got off the hook. Maybe Archie died for the sins of his great-great-grandfather. He seemed to have inherited the same destructive lust for land. They both reneged on a deal in order to keep the place for themselves.'

'The place is jinxed. Perhaps I'll stay put at The Manse. Why don't you see if you can get the Cold Case Unit moved to Bendigo, after all, there is only one of you?'

'I like the "we" bit in all this.' He said and rounded the bench to clink glasses and kiss her lightly.

'The apron suits you. Maybe I could employ you as cook and gardener.'

'Hmm,' he said settling into a lingering kiss. 'What are the terms and conditions like?'

'Not that attractive, I'm afraid. You'd be on call around the clock. Accommodation is provided but you would have to share a room … and I could only pay you in kind.'

'What "kind" of kind?'

'This kind …' She showed him.

ACKNOWLEDGEMENTS

I remain indebted to: Rosemary Sorensen, then Director of *Bendigo Writers Festival*, for editing and for liking my manuscript enough in the first place; Keith Sutherland and Peter Kennedy from *Bendigo Publishing*; and wine writer, Max Allen, for launching that first edition.

Many thanks to: Greg Dedman for masterful firsthand knowledge of local and French winemaking; June Andrew, Stephen Haby and Brian Hinneberg for generously sharing their specialist knowledge; "test-readers" Cameron King and Jennie de Jong; Des Lowry for additional editing; Roger Dunn for manuscript assessment; and Dianne Dempsey and Lyons Architecture.

I am most grateful to Amy Doak of *Accidental Publishing* for re-publishing *A Vintage Death* as a companion title with my follow up novel, *Wetland* in 2018; and to Geoff and Wendy Collishaw from Synchronicity Performing Arts for adapting and performing *A Vintage Death* as a stage play which premiered at Bendigo in 2024.

The creation of Claude Gatineau was inspired by Antoine Fauchery and his self-penned *Letters From a Miner in Australia*, published in Paris in 1857. The English translation was published by Georgian House Melbourne in 1965.

Among the many other publications I consulted for this novel, the following were invaluable: *McIvor A History of the Shire and the Township of Heathcote* by J.O. Randell; *Pastoral Settlement in Northern Victoria Volume 2 the Campaspe District*, also by J.O. Randell; *Victoria Police Fatal Shootings* by Damian Marrett (article on the website, *Do the crime, do the time*); and Oz Clarke's *Australian Wine Companion*.

The Goldfields Research Centre in Bendigo, the Bendigo Regional Archives Centre and the National Library of Australia Trove website also proved to be wonderful sources of local history.